Chrystallia
& THE SOURCE
OF LIGHT

P.M. Glaser

GREENLEAF
BOOK GROUP PRESS

Published by Greenleaf Book Group Press
Austin, Texas
www.gbgpress.com

Distributed by Greenleaf Book Group LLC

For ordering information or special discounts for bulk purchases, please contact Greenleaf Book Group LLC at PO Box 91869, Austin, TX 78709, 512.891.6100.

Character designs and interior illustrations by Dave Zaboski
Design and composition by Peter Green Design
Cover design by Wallen/Green
Cover illustrations by Dominick Domingo

Glaser, Paul Michael.
Chrystallia and The Source of Light / Paul Michael Glaser. -- 1st ed. p. ; cm.

Summary: A life-affirming story about a thirteen-year-old girl and her nine-year-old brother who, on the eve of their last Christmas with their dying mother, take a magical journey through the underground world of crystals and minerals in search of the source of light.
Interest age group: 009-012.

ISBN: 978-1-60832-232-9

1. Brothers and sisters--Juvenile fiction. 2. Light sources--Juvenile fiction. 3. Crystals--Juvenile fiction. 4. Underground areas--Juvenile fiction. 5. Mothers--Death--Juvenile fiction. 6. Christmas--Juvenile fiction. 7. Brothers and sisters--Fiction. 8. Light--Fiction. 9. Crystals--Fiction. 10. Underground areas--Fiction. 11. Mothers--Death--Fiction. 12. Christmas--Fiction. 13. Adventure fiction. 14. Fantasy fiction. I. Title.

PZ7.G4812 Chr 2011
[Fic]   2011927560

Part of the Tree Neutral® program, which offsets the number of trees consumed in the production and printing of this book by taking proactive steps, such as planting trees in direct proportion to the number of trees used: www.treeneutral.com

Printed in the United States of America on acid-free paper
11 12 13 14 15 16   10 9 8 7 6 5 4 3 2 1
First Edition

For Zoë and Jake

Contents

ACKNOWLEDGMENTS

I wouldn't have been able to write *Chrystallia* were it not for all those who came and went in my life. I am only a conduit for the accumulation of them.

I would like to thank my mother, Dorothy, who introduced me to the magic of storytelling. My father, Samuel, who was an example of perseverance and passion and fed my imagination with his world of art and design. My sister Priscilla for the example of her commitment to a personal dream; my sister Constance for her love and the example of her work ethic. My tenth-grade geology teacher, Herma Bierman, who exposed me to the underground world of minerals and crystals; and Whitney Haley, who encouraged me to dream. Gibby Graves, who first took me fishing, and his son, Butch, who taught me to make my own bow and arrows. My deceased wife, Elizabeth, for giving me two beautiful children, and my son, Jake, whose courage and determination constantly amaze me; Tracy for giving me Zoë . . . and Zoë for all that she is.

I would like to thank Robert Strock for everything that he continues to teach me, my friend Robert Cort for being Robert Cort, and Johnny and Bobby and my golfing buddies for witnessing my pursuit of this humbling respite from my writing.

I would like to thank Bill Wallen for teaching us all so much and for seeing the "added value" and being instrumental in making this all come true; Peter Green for his passion, support, and expertise, and Sol Weisel for his help, heart, and commitment.

My gratitude to Tesa Conlin for taking me so gently and patiently back to seventh-grade English, and Rosemary Delderfield for making sure I stayed in class.

Tim Sims and all those at Peter Green Design for their generosity and support.

Dave Zaboski for his friendship, illustrations, and participation in this journey; Dominick Domingo for his timely contribution; Elaine Lasseff for her constant support and assistance; and Pam Meserve for her unflagging dedication . . .

And to all those who have read, and will read, *Chrystallia*, with the hope that we can, indeed, make this a better world.

Chrystallia

& THE SOURCE OF LIGHT

My mother named me Maggie. She called me "Magpie" 'cause I came out squawking so loudly the nurses had to cover their ears. I'll be thirteen years old in three months and six days. I've got freckles, blue eyes, and light brown hair, and my mother tells me I'm not fat. She tells me a lot of things.

My girlfriends say I'm pretty, but they're prettier. I still wear ugly braces on my teeth, and I hated my younger brother, Jesse Cooper, for the first nine years of his life.

Then this incredible thing happened. I'd heard of people believing they had lived another life in a different time, or knowing with dead certainty that something had happened when they had no way of knowing that it had happened — but I'd never heard of this.

Neither have you.

PROLOGUE

I didn't see it in the dark, not at first.

My little brother Jesse stood stock-still in the snow-covered clearing, his quick breath shooting puffs of white steam in the glow of his new flashlight. The chilly gray afternoon had become freezing night in the deep forest, and, thanks to him, we were still searching for our Christmas tree.

He was staring into a family of birch trees, his bright beam reflecting off their black-notched silvery skins then vanishing into the dark woods beyond.

A small wind spout pushed and pulled at their naked white branches as it danced across the crystal drifts blanketing the forest floor.

Then I saw it.

Hiding in the deep shadows behind the thin white trunks, its shoulders heavy with snow, the fir's great piney boughs hung like the massive arms of a lurking animal.

Jesse's beam climbed up the massive frosted shelves and sparkling curtains of icicles, which hid the dark caverns of the under-boughs. It slid up the narrowing branches, past the thinning birch tops, up to the lone spire of the majestic fir, its snowcapped clumps of young green fingers weaving into a single white shoot pointing high into the starless sky.

"What are you looking at?" I casually inquired.

Jesse's surprised face jerked into the glare of my flashlight.

"N-nothing," he protested lamely, yanking his light off his secret and shining its glare in my face. He knew that I could tell he was lying.

I instantly turned and yelled at the flashlight beams that were skewering the dark forest around us. "Over here, over here! We've found our tree!"

"No, we haven't!" Jesse cried.

We did this every year, and every year he always found something wrong with every tree. I wasn't the only one who was cold and miserable and wanted to go home.

"Over here!" I repeated, louder this time. "Jesse's found our tree! Over here!"

Staring daggers at me, Jesse insisted, "No, I haven't!"

I smiled spitefully into the white of his light.

Daddy broke into the clearing, lugging his heavy yellow-and-black chainsaw through the deep snow, with Aunt Doris, Uncle Billy, and our cousin Cody following along on his heels.

Uncle Billy is Daddy's younger brother. He sells tires. He also wears one around his middle and is losing his hair. Aunt Doris has pink cheeks, long blonde braids, and an annoyingly cheerful smile. She looks as if she should be milking cows in Switzerland.

They whistled when they saw the tree.

"You can't cut it down," Jesse whined. "There are trees all around it!"

"There's an opening over here!" called Uncle Billy, circling the stand of birches. "We could fell her through here!"

"Cody!" barked Uncle Billy. "Give us a hand here."

Cody is sixteen and an honors student in science, and would be really cute if he wore contacts. Jesse thinks he walks on water.

"Jesse, you and Maggie stand back," Daddy ordered, crouching beneath the huge limbs.

Daddy is six feet two inches tall, and he never wears a hat. His wavy brown hair was frosted with snow, and in his stained leather gloves, tall boots, and checkered shirt, he looked like a movie star.

Easily hefting the heavy chainsaw, he gave its starter cord a yank. "Shine your lights over here!" he called, his breath steaming in the glare of our flashlights. He yanked again and the chainsaw roared to life. Its shiny blade became a silvery blur, and its motor spewed a billowing cloud of blue smoke that turned our bright crisscrossing beams into magical wands.

Bracing his feet, he raced the chattering motor again and again.

"Please don't!" pleaded Jesse as the saw's teeth tore into the glistening bark and an explosion of birds burst from their icy home in a flurry of snow and flashing feathers.

The wailing whine of the saw suddenly died leaving only the hollow sound of pounding wings slowly disappearing into the quiet night sky.

The steaming blade had frozen, stuck in the tree's green wood, and the smell of burnt oil and pine stained the cold air.

"It's not fair!" Jesse complained as Daddy yanked the chainsaw back to life.

Gunning the motor over and over, he wrestled with the thick trunk to release the saw's blade.

In a flash, the silvery teeth spun free with a howling scream, spitting out a stream of white pulp with a whining snarl.

The saw screamed louder with the second cut. This was the important one because it would determine which way the tree would fall.

A fleshy wedge of white wood squirted from the thick trunk, and the saw's motor fell silent.

The gigantic fir shuddered, and its snowy boughs gently bounced in the icy breeze. Somehow, the magnificent evergreen remained standing, and suddenly I wanted this to have been a horrible mistake. I wanted the tree to regrow its roots and live.

Daddy and Uncle Billy each grabbed a branch.

"On three," coached Uncle Billy. "Watch it, everybody!"

They pulled.

The huge tree leaned farther away.

They pulled harder, and the towering pine hesitated as if it weren't quite sure which way to go.

The wind swirled, and the tree floated back to center. It paused; then its white-capped crest slowly drifted sideways.

It was falling.

Falling, rushing, and crashing through snapping birch branches, the great tree was swallowed up in a silent explosion of snow as my scream died into the wet wool of my icy mittens that I had clamped tightly to my ears.

THE MAGIC TREE

"I never liked Christmas. Everybody going
"Ho-ho-ho" and "Have a Merry, Merry Christmas."
That's not how it felt. Sure, it was full of glittery
lights and snowy nights, but there was something
else, something underneath it all, that didn't feel
good. Something that wouldn't go away, even with
all the pretty decorations and Daddy's warm fire and
Mom's hot chocolate.

Something sad, like when you have to say good-
bye to a close friend and you don't want to.

Something final that was going to come to an
end no matter how hard you wished for it not to.

I sat by myself at the back of Daddy's wagon, feeling cold
and alone.

The others were squeezed in around the sides of the
Christmas tree. Its huge boughs lay across their laps and
softly jounced to the muffled gait of our wagon's mismatched
Clydesdales, Molly and Blue.

Chocolate brown with a misty white blaze, Molly is friskier

and shorter than Blue, who is older and slower, his coat a mottled blue-gray and his mane and tail black.

Snorting steam, they tossed their heads and shook their harness bells. I could tell they were happy to be pulling such a light load. Their usual job is hauling heavier loads of exotic trees like black walnut and silver ash from our forest. Daddy then harvests, dries, and mills the trees to create the beautiful inlaid designs for the furniture he builds.

No more.

This would be the last Christmas tree that would hang out over the back of our wagon and smother us in its piney perfume.

Nobody spoke.

House lights sparkled across the valley, and I could smell a burning fireplace.

I love this valley. I love our house that Daddy built with his own hands. He got the neighboring farmers to help, and we all pitched in, even Uncle Billy.

It took the whole summer to build. I remembered the first night we slept on the ground and stared up at the ceiling of stars silhouetting the crisscrossing beams of our newly raised roof. The crickets kept watch on the night, and Daddy told Mom that we were sleeping in her kitchen, even though Jesse insisted it was the living room because it "felt that way."

I didn't care. For me, all that mattered was that it was our house.

Some idiots at my school said it looked like a wood-and-glass spaceship. Jesse said it looked like a giant crystal, with its twenty-foot ceilings, its sharp spires, and its triangular windows, but what did he know?

Ever since Cody and Jesse found some rocks and minerals inside Indian Tooth, the abandoned silver mine above our house, my annoying little brother had become an "expert" on crystals.

Worse still, Cody gave Jesse a book called *The World Book of Rocks and Minerals* last year, and Jesse became obsessed with crystals and how any shape, color, or texture the human brain could possibly imagine already exists underground.

He said Daddy's design of the house was proof.

Proof of what, I wondered; it doesn't look like a crystal to me. It looks like a collection of wooden pyramids, with its great oak beams and long sloping walls.

Well, it doesn't matter anymore. The Colorado State Bank is kicking us out of our house and there is nothing we can do about it.

Molly whinnied.

"Jesse, I think your mother's going to love this tree," Aunt Doris chirped cheerfully.

Refusing to answer, Jesse sulked, hunched in "his" seat next to Daddy, who flicked the thick reins and quietly clucked to Molly and Blue. Sometimes I find it hard to believe that Jesse and I are brother and sister. He's so different from me, with his green eyes and pointy head, and his belief that there is "something else" out there that you can't see or touch.

Aunt Doris, Uncle Billy, and Cody live two states away and have stayed with us every Christmas for as long as I can remember. This year they came earlier because Mom is getting sicker and Daddy is struggling to take care of her while closing up his business.

We are going to be moving in with them, after.

After. That's how everybody talks about it.

I hate the way everyone is always saying "after" and "when" and never saying the horrible words that follow, but letting their voices trail off like forgotten thoughts. And the way Aunt Doris is trying to connect with Jesse more than ever, knitting him two sweaters this Christmas and bringing him even more of his favorite cookies than she had before.

Cody gave Jesse yet another book, *The Alchemy of Crystals*, that tells about all the mystical things people believed crystals could do, like healing and telling the future. Now all Jesse talks about are the "magical properties" of crystals, and the special relationship that humans have with crystals and minerals that can turn lead into gold with the power of the heart. Jesse and Cody spend hours and hours in Jesse's room searching for magical ways to save Mom. That's all he believes in, that and finding a way to keep us from moving.

Me? I refuse to believe in anything. My world had changed so much since Jesse was born that whenever anything bad happens, I think it's just my luck.

Like when Dr. Fresnel sat with Daddy, Jesse, and me in the ugly green hospital waiting room, with its orange chairs and smell of disinfectant and sick people.

While he was quietly explaining that there was nothing more they could do for Mom and that this third visit was going to be her last, Jesse kept this real stony look on his face as if he were trying to keep the words from getting in.

I had already figured out that she was dying. You could just look at her sunken blue eyes and wispy hair and see that she was wasting away.

Then one day I caught her and Daddy talking quietly in their bedroom about us moving in with Aunt Doris and Uncle Billy, "after."

Daddy was sitting on the edge of the beautiful bed he had built for them, and Mom was propped up against the headboard, which fanned out behind her like the rays of a setting sun. It was inlaid with an intricate design of dark- and light-colored woods, which if you looked really closely, resembled a portrait of each one of us.

Daddy was crying and Mom was holding his hand, and then I was standing in the doorway asking, "Why?"

That's all I kept saying: "Why?"

As if she were talking about the weather, Mom kept trying to explain that not enough people were buying Daddy's wonderful furniture and that's why the bank was recalling our loan that had let us buy the land and build our house. Besides, Uncle Billy's home was only temporary and only two states away.

Then she reached out to me with her thin arms.

I couldn't go to her.

I couldn't move.

My chest hurt, and my throat was a burning knot, and when she said that it was really important to be careful how we told Jesse—that we needed to take care of Jesse because Jesse was so young and Jesse couldn't understand these things—I burst out crying and yelled that it was *always* all about Jesse! What about me? What about my feelings?

And I turned and ran from their room.

It took us forever to decorate the tree.

Jesse refused to help, so Cody and I got out the ladders and put up the crystal balls and colored lights while Mom dozed beneath her purple comforter on the couch.

Uncle Billy was cooking his favorite—tuna casserole with baked beans—and it was stinking up the entire house. Daddy was still in his woodshop.

We were practically finished with the tree when Jesse came clomping down the split-log staircase carrying three sloppily wrapped gifts.

"Oh, look, it's Santa!" I teased, dropping silver tinsel on his pinhead as he placed two of his gifts beneath the tree. "Jesse still believes in Santa."

Brushing off the tinsel, Jesse carried his third present over to Mom and carefully sat on the edge of the couch.

She gently pushed the hair from his eyes as she always did. "It's a beautiful tree, Jesse," she said softly.

"Jesse didn't want us to cut it down," I told her. "He said it was *special*."

"It *is* special," Mom affirmed, once again taking Jesse's side.

She's always taking Jesse's side.

"It didn't want to be cut down!" Jesse pouted. "Besides, why do we need such a big tree?"

"Jesse had a conversation with the tree," I joked, dropping tinsel on Cody's head.

"Why do you have to be such a loser?" Jesse whined.

Mom sighed. "Do you think you two could sign a truce for maybe one night?"

"Why are you putting so much tinsel on it?" Jesse complained.

"Because it's Christmas, dummy," I chirped, tossing another handful on the tree. "More is better."

Grumbling sourly, Jesse demanded, "What's so special about having a Christmas tree anyway?"

Mom smiled and gave him a weak hug. "You love Christmas trees, Jesse!" she reminded him as he continued to sulk. "You know," she confided, "I've often thought that when our ancestors found themselves living in the northernmost climes, where it was dark twenty-four hours a day in the dead of winter, they must have lived in fear that the light would never return.

"So they chose a plant that was always green—the 'evergreen' tree—and decorated it with things to eat and symbols of life as an offering to the light so that it would return."

"Well, we have electricity," Jesse grouched. "And we know the light will return."

"It's not about electricity," Mom explained patiently. "And there's a big difference between what we know and what we fear."

Ever since we were old enough to understand words, Mom had told us stories of magical children, animals, kings, queens, and dragons. When I was little, I believed in all that stuff, but after Jesse was born, I found them just plain boring. I thought it was a bad joke on people who needed something to believe in.

Jesse was nine, though, and he still believed. He and Mom would sit in the kitchen for hours having big discussions about why things happened.

Daddy and I were more alike. We only trusted what was right in front of us, what we could hold on to and see.

Jesse handed Mom the gift he had for her.

Smiling softly, she sighed, "Can't this wait till morning?"

I knew she was tired and wanted to rest, but Jesse stubbornly shook his head.

"There are other gifts for tomorrow," he insisted.

Studying him, she mused, "You're a funny boy." And taking a moment to collect her strength, she carefully undid Jesse's sloppy bow and wrinkled wrapping paper as though they were as valuable as the gift itself.

Holding up a chunk of purple-and-white crystals she exclaimed, "It's beautiful, Jesse!" Then a look of concern crossed her face. "Where did you get it?" she asked, as if she didn't already know.

We all knew. He'd gotten it from Indian Tooth Mine— where he wasn't supposed to go.

Ignoring the question, Jesse gushed, "It's amethyst! It's over nine hundred million years old! Amethyst is the most healing of all the crystals. They say it carries the female energy of the Moon and is an excellent stone for meditations—"

"I'll keep it right next to my bed, Jesse," Mom assured him.

"It likes seawater and cold . . ." his voice rising, "and is the best for the sixth chakra, the 'crown' chakra, and . . ."

Closing her eyes, Mom insisted tiredly, "I'm fine, Jesse."

"No, you're not!" he blurted.

There was an embarrassed silence as Cody shifted uncomfortably on his ladder. I could have killed Jesse.

Mom took his hand and confided quietly, "Jesse . . . do you know what my daddy used to say to me? 'Wherever we find ourselves, we're there for a reason, even if the only reason is that that's where we find ourselves.'"

"Well, riddles aren't going to make you better!" Jesse protested, not caring that everyone was listening.

Slowly shaking her head, she whispered, "No, they aren't. But they can help with your fear."

You could tell she hated having to treat him like an adult when he was still such a baby.

Gently admonishing him, she weakly held up the piece of

amethyst. "This is very beautiful, Jesse . . . but what did we say about not going into the mine?"

"He's not supposed to," I reminded her, "but that doesn't stop him."

Jesse got away with everything.

Mom gave me a disapproving glance as Uncle Billy appeared in the doorway wearing an apron and a spatula.

"I hope everybody's as hungry as I am!" he announced enthusiastically.

Nobody budged.

Oblivious to everyone's look of panic at the mention of his awful cooking, Uncle Billy disappeared back into the kitchen, yelling, "Jesse, go get your old man."

Mom gave Jesse a playful nudge. "Go on, mister," she urged, "and promise me that's the last time you go into that mine. It's unsafe."

Jesse reluctantly nodded, picked himself up, and shuffled out of the room.

Mom wouldn't stop looking at me.

"What?" I snapped.

Slowly shaking her head, she sighed, "Jesse just wants to believe, sweetheart. Is it so hard for you to believe?"

"I don't know," I shot back. "What's it gotten you?"

I would have given anything to have taken back those words.

Smiling sadly, mom closed her eyes and lay back on her pillow.

I felt ashamed and angry.

I wanted to disappear.

"I'll never believe! In anything!" I cried. "Never! Ever!"

And I flew up the stairs.

I dreamt of moonlit clouds.

Their shadows drifted silently over our snow-covered valley as the wind whipped and whistled, and an occasional light twinkled in the distance.

I dreamt of Jesse asleep, curled up on his bed in the dirty BMX jacket he practically lived in. He was clenching a chunk of purple amethyst crystals in one hand and his magnifying glass in the other. His crystal and gem books were flung open about his Boy Scout blanket like a meandering castle wall.

I dreamt of his desk and shelves covered with their mess of glittering geodes mixed with rocks of all shapes and sizes. Pieces of petrified wood, fossils, and flint arrowheads were scattered about, and his collection of model airplanes dangled suspended from the ceiling as long shadows of the knights and kings on his chessboard attacked the skateboarders that flew through icy blue skies on the posters tacked to his sloping walls.

He didn't feel the house move.

He didn't feel it roll as if atop the swell of a slow-moving wave.

He didn't feel his bed slide two inches.

It was the half globe of a crystal geode crashing onto the floor that made his eyes pop open.

At first he couldn't make sense of his model airplanes lazily swinging back and forth in the blur above him.

The house groaned and moved again, and several more rocks clattered to the floor and Jesse sat bolt upright in panic.

Then Jesse was shaking my shoulder and blasting his new flashlight in my half-opened eye.

"Maggie! Maggie! Did you feel that?" Jesse whispered wetly in my ear.

"What the—!" I rasped, trying to push the blinding light out of my face. "You scared me, you idiot!"

"Did you feel it?" he demanded, not caring about anything but himself.

"I was sleeping, and no, I didn't! Whatever 'it' was."

Grabbing my arm, he stuck his smelly face into mine. "The house!" he spluttered, spraying me with a shower of saliva. His eyes were wide in the moonlight. "It moved! Didn't you feel it move?"

Had I? In my dream, yes . . . but was I still dreaming?

Jesse was listening for something. For what?

"What?" I demanded, shaking off his hand.

He shushed me and kept listening.

Flopping angrily onto my back, I yanked the covers over my head and snarled, "Get out of my room or I'm going to call Daddy!"

I could see his flashlight beam drilling at the inside of my blanket.

"It moved! I was in bed and—"

I sat straight up. "I don't want to play! Okay?" I hissed.

His mouth kept opening and closing like he was a fish out of water.

Disgusted, I lay back down.

"I'm not leaving till you come and look," he threatened.

I sat back up so quickly I nearly knocked him over.

"You're gonna be sooo sorry!" I promised him.

Stepping into my boots, I pulled on my winter jacket—we couldn't afford to heat the house at night even though Mom had insisted we keep the Christmas tree lights on—and angrily followed Jesse to the top of the stairs.

He was shining his flashlight into the living room below.

Everything looked normal to me.

"You're so dead," I said, turning to go back to bed. "I'm going—"

"Wait!" he cried, grabbing my sleeve.

"Ow! What're you doing?" I yelped.

"Look!" he squeaked, pointing his flashlight at a pile of gifts stacked beneath the blinking lights of the Christmas tree.

"Oh, look, it must've been Santa!" I smirked.

"No, LOOK!" Jesse insisted, jabbing his flashlight beam at a large green box with a wide red ribbon around it.

The box jiggled a little, moved sideways, and slowly slid off a smaller blue box.

"Did you see that?"

"See what? The box moved," I pointed out, knowing it didn't make any sense. "Maybe it's a new pet or something."

Then it moved again.

"That!" Jesse exclaimed and started down the stairs.

Seizing the arm of his jacket, I demanded, "What are you doing!"

"Goin' to look!" he snapped, snatching his arm back and leaving me standing alone on the staircase.

"We shouldn't even be up!" I whispered loudly as I stumbled after him. "Those are our Christmas presents!" I had a bad feeling inside, and I just wanted to go back to bed.

Stopping two feet from the big green box, Jesse took a breath and then nudged it with his toe.

Nothing happened.

"I'm going back to bed," I announced.

He pushed it again, harder.

This time the box slid to the side and my heart nearly leapt out of my chest. Underneath the box, the tree had . . . regrown its roots through the floor!

This had to be a dream.

Large twisting roots wound around the dead trunk and then plunged into and through Daddy's hardwood floor!

"They go right through the floor!" Jesse exclaimed, pointing out the obvious.

"Look!" he squealed, pointing at a large, gaping hole between two of the twisting roots. Getting down on his knees, he crawled closer.

"Jesse!" I rasped.

It was as if he were still in diapers, crawling after anything that caught his curiosity—which was usually everything.

Stumbling down the stairs, I crept up behind him and peeked over his shoulder.

The yawning hole disappeared into complete darkness!

Squeezing my eyes shut, I silently prayed, *This is a dream, this is a dream . . .*

When I opened my eyes, Jesse was leaning out over the edge of the hole!

"Jesse!"

"Helloooo?" he softly called into the abyss.

We held our breath and listened. There was nothing, not even an echo.

Jesse pointed his flashlight down into the hole, and the beam of light dove into the black emptiness and disappeared.

Jesse turned off his flashlight and a shiver flew up my spine.

"There … There!" I blurted.

Twinkling far below us was a pinprick of light that seemed to be getting brighter.

Then it became two lights, and they were both getting brighter, and bigger! *Oh my God!* I thought. *They're coming toward us!*

I wanted to stand up and run. *Please, Mommy and Daddy, make me wake up! Please let me wake up!* I couldn't move.

The lights were getting closer and larger . . . Then they just stopped and floated there in the black chasm beneath us.

I blinked and shook my head.

The lights were changing shape!

They were growing eyes . . . and mouths! They were becoming faces!

Two bodiless faces were looking up at us and watching us as if they were studying us.

The one that was staring at me seemed familiar.

Then it smiled.

It was me!

It was *my* face—my own face staring back at me!

I couldn't breathe. Petrified, I got to my feet. The room began to spin. I took a step. . .

But there was nothing beneath me!

I had stepped into the hole ... into the faces ... I was falling!

I screamed, and suddenly everything slowed.

There was Jesse's outstretched hand! It took an eternity to reach for it, then it was sliding away, and his mouth was opening in a silent scream.

He was falling as well!

Our echoing screams doubled and redoubled as we fell through brilliant ribbons and tubes of colored light!

"Jesse . . . esseee . . . esseee!!"

"Aggie . . . Maaaggiee . . . ggieee!!"

Snaking streams of light spiraled up and around us like an endless helix of DNA molecules.

Images began to appear and spin past us. Images of people and places: recess at school, our unfinished house, Mommy and Daddy wearing birthday hats. And there were sounds! Sounds of laughter, a baby crying, horses neighing. There were more images: Nick at Nite, the Teletubbies, the 9/11 Towers collapsing; Mom holding us, playing with us, laughing, tickling us.

Turning 'round and 'round as we fell, each time I saw Jesse he looked younger, and smaller! He was eight years old, then five, then two. He was becoming a baby!

I looked down at my own hands. They had become small and pink and wrinkly!

There were still more images . . . and sounds: Fireworks, and family picnics, a boat rocking in a storm . . . the moon and stars, baby chickens pecking at my toes . . . rushing water, Jesse's first steps . . . Mom leaning over me with a bottle.

There was a face with a doctor's mask and a blur of eyes peering down at me . . . then nothing!

Nothing but blackness.

And silence.

CHRYSTALLIA

I remember, when I was little, before my brother was born, my mother took me into a sunny meadow where the air smelled sweet and the flowers danced to birdsong.

Holding on to her strong fingers, I ran to keep up with her long legs as the tall grass slapped and stung at my sunburned skin.

We came to a sparkling stream that rushed and burbled 'round and over its rocks. Shadows scattered across the sunlit bottom, and the riverbank sand was warm beneath my bare feet.

Mom lifted me onto a large fallen tree, and a beautiful dragonfly landed beside me on the dry gray wood.

It shimmered gold and green, and its glittering purple wings flickered in the bright sun.

Holding my breath, I carefully reached to touch it . . .

It darted away across the sliding water and

suddenly, something was climbing up through sparkling spray.

Suspended in sunlight — its pink-and-silver belly twisting atop a wide dark tail, a huge shiny fish had snatched my tinsel-green dragonfly in its yellow-spotted jaws!

There was a crashing splash . . . and the ferocious fish vanished in a swirl of bubbles.

A sunlit cloud of mayflies dove into the dark shade.

A bird complained.

My magic dragonfly was no more.

I cried.

I cried and cried, and my mother held me in her strong arms, gently crushing me to her warm hair and sweet smell.

I could hear the roar of my heartbeat.

I couldn't see anything.

I couldn't feel anything.

Had I stopped falling?

Was I still dreaming?

"Jesse?" I whispered and my voice exploded into a scatter of echoes that rolled over and through each other into pitch-black silence.

I felt something—something beneath me! It was cold and hard.

"Jesse!" I hissed again, and my echoing voice was joined by his: "Maggiee . . . Jesseee . . . aggie . . . esseee . . ."

I couldn't tell where he was!

"Where are you, Jesse?"

"Over here . . . eere . . . eere," his voice called.

"Over where?"

"Erre . . . wherrre . . . erre," our echoes tumbling away until all I could hear was my own breathing.

CLICK!

A blinding white beam shot over my head.

Craaack!

The beam ricocheted off something and split in two.

CRAAACK! CRAAACK!

The two beams became four, eight—doubling and redoubling, shooting and shattering streaks of light in every color imaginable into an exploding chaos of noise.

I could see Jesse!

He was nine years old again, his eyes squeezed shut and covering his ears with his blazing flashlight still clutched in one hand.

I closed my eyes, covered my ears and screamed.

Everything became quiet and still.

Jesse had turned off his flashlight, and the storm of ricocheting light beams had fallen onto a distant horizon, where jagged flashes of lightning exploded inside rumbling angular clouds as they roiled and rolled into and through each other.

Around us—all around us as far as the eye could see—crystals and minerals of all shapes and sizes throbbed and pulsed with a calliope of color, spraying and radiating thin shafts, thick streaks, floating mists, and great splashes of brilliance.

Spreading out before us, a sea of deep greens was punctuated by sparkling yellows, feathery oranges, and wispy whites.

Shimmering cobwebs glistened green and gold, and brilliant red crystal spikes pin-cushioned soft cubes of blue.

"Where are we?" I croaked, my face numb and my ears ringing. My scalp felt on fire.

It was as if we were inside a rainbow made of crystals. Some were angular, some round, some covered with glittering minerals. Lacey lines of silver wrapped around and pierced clusters of crystals, erupting into countless spiny white bundles that blossomed with miniature rainbows.

"These are all c-crys . . . these are c-crystals!" Jesse stammered. "Crystals and minerals!"

Thin blades of light sparked and spat off mica-skinned slabs that loomed above them.

Brilliant streaks of blue-and-green light shot from jagged columns of blue and green crystal thrusting from crusty sleeves of rock.

"Where are we, Jesse?" I asked in a squeaking whisper. "Are we in the mine?"

Playfully circling my feet, a froth of gold bubbles streamed a mane of silvery blue hair and snaked away with needly black clusters of crystals riding its back.

"I don't know," Jesse whispered, picking up a glowing orange chunk whose sparks of light spat through thousands of tiny crystal windows.

"Holy tomoleee!" he suddenly exclaimed, quickly stuffing it into his pocket and picking up a brilliant blue one.

Peering into a large bank of yellow crystals, I could see the shattered and scattered reflections of my face in the fractured facets.

"Hey, look!" Jesse yelped, leaning over a similar bank that pulsed with tiny explosions of red-and-white rippling light. "I can see hundreds of myself!" he cried excitedly, waving at his reflections like an idiot.

"Jesse, we don't know where we are! Where are we?"

"I don't know! Okay?" he snapped, turning back to wave at himself. "I don't have a clue whe—"

He stared into the bank of red-and-white quartz, his mouth hanging open.

"Jesse?"

He was just pointing dumbly at the reddish crystals in front of him.

Disgusted, I marched over and impatiently pushed him aside.

Among the tiny clusters and spinning strings of red-and-white light, I could see noses, smiling mouths, and pairs of eyes watching me, looking at me.

Only they weren't *my* noses and eyes.

They were *Jesse's*!

I was looking at Jesse's face smashed into a thousand pieces—and they were smiling and waving as many hands at me while Jesse was standing right next to me, not waving either of his hands.

Oh God! I thought, watching in horror as small sprays of pink-and-red light began erupting from hundreds of fingers.

A multitude of arms and legs started twisting and stretching through an endless geometry of crisscrossing lines that were streaking with light.

Hundreds of hands were reaching—toward me!

Jesse's reflections were swimming up at me from beneath the crystal surface.

"Look!" cried Jesse, and there was a sudden burst of light.

I covered my eyes as an explosion of tiny crystals peppered my hands and face.

Petrified, I peeked.

Jesse's reflection was standing outside the bank of crystals!

Sprays of pink light shot from its crystal eyes, mouth, knees, and elbows! Waves of red-and-white light pulsed from its chest, and thin shards of lightning raced helter-skelter along splitting and splintering facets throughout its entire body.

It was a perfect replica of Jesse.

Staggering, it seemed to be trying to find its balance.

"Okay, I gotta breathe," Jesse blurted.

A burst of red light came out of the reflection's mouth with a gravelly "Okaaay-I-gotttabreeethe!"

"Jesse?" I squealed.

Turning to me, the reflection screeched like fingernails on a blackboard. "Jesss-ssseeeee!"

"It-it talks!" exclaimed Jesse.

"Iiiit-taaalks," the creature mimicked.

"You talk!" Jesse blurted. "But you're . . . you're quartz and . . . and pyrope!"

"Quaarrtss-n-pyyrrrope!" Jesse's reflection replied, its voice becoming more and more like Jesse's.

"What's pyrope?" I asked, wondering why I even cared.

"It's red crystal garnet," Jesse whispered excitedly. "Its red color comes from the mineral pyrope. The Greeks believed it was a symbol of faith and light."

The pyrope thing kept pointing at him.

"Quartz-nn-pyyrope," it rasped again, pronouncing the words even better.

Shaking his head, Jesse jabbed his own chest with his finger. "No. I'm Jesse," he explained, enunciating carefully, "Jes-se. You are quartz and pyrope." Then he pointed at me. "And she's Maa-ggie," he said, as if he were talking to some exchange student.

The pyrope thing stuck a crystal finger in my direction. "An-shees-Maa-ggeee!" it blurted in a shower of pink light.

"Jesse! What are you doing?" I cried, stamping my foot in frustration. This had to be a nightmare. I had to wake up.

Another voice screeched.

"JESSSEEE-WHAT-RRR-YOO-DOOIINNG?"

I jumped a mile.

Standing behind me, *my* reflection was stamping its foot and pointing at me just like I was pointing at her!

"OH MY GOD!" I gasped, stumbling backward.

"Ohh-mmyy-Godd!" it mimicked, stumbling backward as well, streaking spines of yellow light flashing through its shivering shape.

Eyes wide, Jesse yammered, "You're scheelite! You're yellow scheelite!"

"Yellloww-sheeelite!" the pyropey thing chimed in.

"Wh-what's schee-scheelite?" I stammered.

"It's a crystal!" Jesse gushed. "A rare crystal from China that is said to help you have insight and balance." He looked incredulously from me to my reflection. "Look at her! She looks just like you!"

Turning back to the scheelite thing, Jesse patiently introduced himself. "I'm Jes-se," he enunciated carefully, then pointed at me again, "and she's Maa-ggie."

"Jesse! You're talking to rocks!" I screamed. I had to be dreaming. I wanted to be home. I wanted to be back in bed, with none of this happening to me!

The scheelite aimed a flashing finger at me. "Mc-geee!" she squeaked shyly.

"MAGGIE!" I snapped at her.

Scheelite's yellow light shot off in all directions. She started to shake, and the lines of her crystal face got all scrunched up as if she were going to cry.

I'd had enough of this. "I want to get out of here, Jesse! Now! How do we get out of here?" I demanded.

Then another voice, deep and gravelly, rumbled, "Howw-doo-wee-get-outta-heere?"

As if two of these things weren't enough, a shorter, fatter version of Jesse stomped up and down on two fat feet as though it had just come in from the snow. It was made of glittering green-and-black crystals with squiggly yellow lines vibrating all over its surface.

Struggling to climb out from under the green-and-black clomping feet, a dirty pile of orange-and-purple crystals crackled with streaks of angry orange light.

"Gett-offa-my-baack, Hornbee!" it snarled in a brassy voice. It had the body of a female wrestler and a really fat version of my face.

"You're hornblende, aren't you?" my brother yipped in delight at the stomper. "You're used with sugilite to give peace of mind and protect the wearer from evil!"

Hornbee reminded me of Jesse when he was still in diapers.

Turning to the female wrestler, Jesse continued his geology lesson. "And you're pegmatite! You're the 'birth rock' of crystals from hydrothermal veins!"

"PEG!" the wrestler corrected him with a nasty growl.

Her angry streaks of purple-and-orange light attacked Hornbee's rippling glitter and she gave him a shove.

Falling backward, he nearly crushed me. "You're McGee? I'm Hornbee," he rasped in my face with a rush of foul yellow light.

"Maggie!" I yelled at him. "Okay? Maag-gie! Not McGee!"

Now *I* was talking to rocks!

Peg sneered at Hornbee. "You're ugly," she cracked.

"You're fat," Hornbee snorted.

Slouching and sliding like a runway model, a thin stack of red, blue, and green crystals with orange hair—which was made of crystals, too—came slinking in. She reminded me of a rainbow Popsicle and didn't look anything at all like me, except maybe for her eyes when I borrowed Mom's mascara.

"Tourmaline!" Jesse exclaimed.

"Y'all can call me Torri . . . hunny," she purred in a slow Southern drawl, her multicolored light rippling through her like a flickering neon sign. "Sweet . . . preshuss . . . Torri."

"You're the gemstone of love and friendship!" Jesse cried, as if she were a long-lost cousin.

Flickering with fascination, Hornbee stumbled into Torri, knocking off a piece of her crystal arm.

"Oh dea-ah! Mah ahm!" she cried with a splash of light.

Peg snorted, "You're just too soft, hunny," she grated, clearly jealous.

Pyrope couldn't take his eyes off the Torri Popsicle. "She's a gem," he whispered loudly.

A black bundle of sticklike crystals marched up to Pyrope and stuck a very large chin in his face. It had red stripes running down its muscular arms, and it reminded me of Jesse when he used to play soldier.

"Who are you?" it barked at Pyrope like a drill sergeant.

"I am Pyrope," Pyrope replied, speaking clearly now, his voice lower and more airy than Jesse's. "Who are you?"

The drill sergeant looked stuck for an answer.

"You're realgar!" Jesse answered victoriously and gave himself a fist pump. "Yes!" he hissed. "You're used to make fireworks!" he bragged, proud of all this useless information.

Relieved to know who he was, the drill sergeant pivoted and pinned Pyrope with a snarling "Reeel-garrr!"

"We're all real," Hornbee claimed.

Confused, Peg growled, "We're all what? I didn't even know I was here until . . ."

"Until . . ." repeated Hornbee.

"Until . . . ?" asked Peg.

"Until?" tried Realgar.

That's when it dawned on me.

It was the light!

It was Jesse's light! These creatures didn't know they existed till Jesse turned on his flashlight!

"Until the light!" I blurted.

"What's 'laaght'?" drawled Torri.

I grabbed Jesse. "Turn on the flashlight! Show them!"

But Jesse couldn't stop gawking at them.

"We've discovered a whole world of crystals!" he muttered in awe.

"Turn on the flashlight!" I yelled, and Jesse held it up like he'd just landed on the moon. "I name this world, 'Chrystallia!'" he declared, and turned it on.

The explosion of ricocheting light beams sent Hornbee and Peg diving for cover.

Shivering luxuriously, Torri stared in awe at her scrambling colors as Pyrope and Scheelite blazed nearly white.

Jesse turned off the flashlight, and the storm immediately retreated onto a flashing horizon, and voices began shouting,

"Whoo-diid-thaat?" "Get-offa-mee!" "Whaat's-goinn'-onn?"

His skin crackling with small explosions of yellow light, Hornbee asked in awe, "What was that?"

"Light," answered Jesse.

"Lliight," grunted Realgar, attacking a rash of red crystals covering his chest.

"Ooooh! Ah'm so fuull of laaght!" Torri cooed, her neon colors flooding into each other.

Smacking her sizzling lips, Peg rolled her muscular shoulders at Realgar as rays of orange-and-purple light burst from her nose and ears. "That was mmm-mmm!" she hummed hungrily.

Realgar pointed a red-hot finger at the flashlight. "That's light?" he growled.

"It's a flashlight. It makes light," Jesse explained, distracted by the voices that were growing louder.

"Heymann-watchit-you're-scratchinmee!" "Ooooh-whaat-color-you-caall-thaaat?"

Pushing past spiky green creatures and teetering columns of metallic yellow cubes, two blue-legged things veered sideways, jerked about by their own ricocheting light as they lurched toward us.

Totally oblivious to them, Pyrope asked, "What's 'light'?"

"It, uh, it lets you see," Jesse replied, staring at his flashlight.

"See? See what?" demanded Realgar, sticking out his chin as if he were posing for a picture.

Tiny explosions of orange-and-purple light popping all over her, Peg leaned into Realgar seductively. "Well, I see you, honey, and you are pretty!" she rasped huskily, then wheeled on Jesse. "I want some more of that light!"

"Me too!" whistled Hornbee, zapping Torri with his crackling glitter.

Torri blushed green.

"Give-us-light! Give-us-light!" more voices cried. The half-formed crystal creatures were getting closer!

"Jesse?" I cried in alarm.

Jesse wasn't even looking at them. He just kept staring at his flashlight.

I reached to take it away from him, but he jerked it back.

"You don't understand," he sputtered and held it up for the creatures to see. "It's just a flashlight! It runs on batteries!" he yelled.

Suddenly erupting from the ground, a huge boulder with black-and-white splotches rose until it towered over us like a giant monster clothed in shimmering mica skin. Pivoting on massive legs, it peered down at us and rumbled, "SHOW ME DA LIGHT!"

"Give them the light, Jesse!" I cried, grabbing for the flashlight. "Turn it on, idiot! Give them their stupid light."

"No!" Jesse cried, pulling it away and sticking it inside his jacket.

"You've got to," I insisted.

"No!" he shouted. "They'll just want more light. Batteries die!"

I cried out as a sharp pain ran down my arm. A silvery chunk of something whizzed past my head.

Stepping in front of me, Jesse started waving his arms. "Don't!" he pleaded. "Stop!"

Stepping in front of Jesse, Pyrope mimicked, "Don't! Stop!"

Something collided with Pyrope's shoulder. He peered curiously at the jagged hole left in his crystal skin.

"They're going to kill us!" I screamed at Jesse. "Give them their stupid light!"

Grabbing Pyrope, Jesse shouted in panic, "How do we get out of here?"

Pyrope was confused. "Out of here?"

More crystals and rocks flew past. The creatures were getting closer.

Hornbee, Peg, Realgar, and the mica-skinned monster ran at them, retaliating with their own crystal missiles.

"Out!" Jesse yelled. "We've got to get out!"

Pyrope shook his head as Scheelite and Torri began throwing rocks at the attacking creatures.

"We've gotta go someplace, someplace else!" Jesse demanded.

"'Place'? What is 'place'?" asked Pyrope.

"*This* place!" Jesse screamed impatiently. He pointed at Pyrope. "You're in that place"—he then pointed at himself—"I'm in this place"—and then at the creatures—"and they're coming from that place to get to the flashlight in this place. C'mon, Pyrope," Jesse pleaded, "there's gotta be another place where we can go!"

Grabbing the cord around Jesse's neck, I yanked the flashlight from his jacket pocket.

"Here! Here's more light!" I screamed and pushed the button.

Swooning in the erupting light storm, Torri latched on to Pyrope's arm as he tried to hold on to Scheelite.

"Pyrope!" Jesse screamed, grabbing his arm. "Don't you have a leader? A president? A king—?"

Suddenly everything went white.

THE KINGDOM OF BERYL

I had a baby brother!

He smelled brand-new, and he weighed next to nothing.

Mom had promised that I could hold him when they got home from the hospital, and here he was, and I was trying really hard not to squeeze him too tight.

He was staring up at me and making bubbles with his mouth.

Laughing, I turned and caught my foot under the corner of the rug.

Suddenly I was falling!

I could see myself as I fell; my mouth was open, and I knew I was holding Jesse too tight.

I landed on my back as Jesse's baby body bounced against mine and everything went still . . . horribly still.

Rooted to the floor, their mouths open in shock, Mom and Dad stared down at us in disbelief.

Jesse started screaming, and Mom snatched him from my arms and, holding him to her, kept telling him over and over that he was all right as she bustled him into the kitchen.

Daddy kept asking, "Is he all right? Is he all right?"

Glancing down at me, he hurriedly asked if I was okay.

I nodded, my eyes wide with fear, but Daddy could always tell when I insisted that I was okay and really wasn't.

Sighing, he reached down and helped me to my feet as I desperately tried not to cry.

"It's okay, Magpie, it's okay," he assured me as he anxiously stared after Mom and Jesse. "Let's go see Jesse," he urged, taking my shaking hand. "C'mon, let's go see Jesse!"

He gave me a little tug, then pulled me after him.

All I wanted was to be held.

A zillion spots of light darted and danced into a bottomless blue expanse beneath my feet.

It was a smooth crystal floor, and the reflected images of Jesse, Pyrope, Scheelite, and Torri were reflected beside mine.

Only they weren't looking down at their reflections; they were staring out at something, mesmerized.

I looked up.

Straining to see past rows of glinting black-and-gray Guards, a crowd of medieval Princes and Princesses, Lords and Ladies, all made of crystals and minerals, were pointing and gawking at us in a great hall!

It was more than a hall. Towering blue-and-green crystal columns throbbed brightly. Their light raced along razor-thin edges that arched up to a glowing crystal dome, which sprayed thin shafts of light onto the crowded crystal court below.

The crystal people were in as many shapes and sizes as there were colors. As with Pyrope, Scheelite, and Torri, pulsing light emanated from their chests into their heads, arms, and legs, making their faceted lines look like skeletons reflecting their own light in a scatter of mirrors beneath their surfaces. Mini–mineral formations glittered and glowed in metallic clumps as crystalline strings, hard angular lines, and soft curves circled through and around their crystal bodies.

The Guards wore massive rock helmets that completely covered their heads, their mica-flecked chests bursting with thin sprays of red light as they stood at attention beneath streaks of yellow light shooting from the glowing tips of their long black lances.

"AHEM!" declared a voice that echoed throughout the great hall.

Two Guards held a man of dull brown crystals to his knees.

Leaking sparks of sputtering light from his trembling elbows and fingers, the brown man cowered before a tall angular red man, who stared at us as he stood over the kneeling figure.

The red man's powerful transparent legs boiled with irregular explosions of light, and his huge head was a crystal triangle of vertical and diagonal lines that converged on a bright star glinting in his forehead. His green eyes smoldered in black holes and the gouged surface of his angular body looked like battered armor. Draped in a purple cape that rippled with a whisper-thin weave of brilliant gold veins, he grasped a gnarled tubular formation of minerals and crystals with a claw-like hand.

White light shot from either end of the crude handle and danced along the jagged edges of two opposing crystal blades; one arched back to slice, its brilliant tip floating high in the air above the red man, while its razored twin curved forward like a hovering scythe, quivering above the brown man's bowed head.

"They're . . . they're not dressed!" someone cried out.

I looked to my right. Noblewomen and Ladies-in-Waiting gasped, their pulsing faces peeking from behind spiny pink-and-blue crystal fans that blushed with soft violet light.

Alarmed to discover that they weren't "dressed," Pyrope, Scheelite, and Torri didn't know what parts of them to cover first.

Erupting in a rush of whispers, the crystal crowd cried out, "What are they?" and "Where did they come from?"

"Look!" Jesse whispered excitedly.

At the top of a wide white staircase that vibrated with a scribble of silvery veins, a crystal blue man with a jutting blue jaw, potbelly, and thin arms and legs was struggling to keep from sliding off a large throne of white quartz and chunks of gold.

Radiating sputtering streaks of gold light, he appeared to be an ancient warrior who had outgrown his chipped and scarred armor. His too-small crystal cape glimmered dimly with a scatter of silver streaks, and his clear green crown fell across his sparkling eyes. He held on to a tall transparent blue staff etched with gold lines. It flickered with blue light pulsing from his cracked crystal hand and resembled a giant ruler.

Beside him, a very thin green woman with a long face and yellowy cat's eyes hovered at the edge of a twisted throne of silvery ore and inspected us like a snake smelling its prey. Throbbing deep inside her, a golden web of spidery thin lines spat out shimmering spikes of yellow light as a green crystal cloak coiled at her ear as if it were listening from behind her clear blue crown, which was trapped in a tangle of silver tendrils sprouting from her hoary head.

This had to be a nightmare. I had to wake up!

"What happened? Where are we?" I whispered to Jesse.

The woman's long green claw of a hand clenched a red crystal leash that was attached to a pile of metallic blocks teetering at her feet. It looked like a small twisted man!

His chipped cubes kept changing from silver to gold and back again. One of his eyes was red, the other green, and they chased after his nose as it kept changing its position on his face. His hands and feet looked like spilled silver syrup, and a smaller version of his own head sat on top of a multicolored crystal stick that he held shakily in front of him.

Turning to Pyrope, Jesse squeaked, "How did we—how, how did you . . . ?"

His light rippling rapidly, Pyrope looked as puzzled as everybody else. "You said K-King . . . Is this 'K-King'?" he stuttered in confusion.

The tall muscular red man with the two-bladed sword cleared his throat. "AHEMMM!" he repeated angrily.

Ignoring him, Jesse blurted at Pyrope, "You mean you . . . You just thought 'King' and this . . . this just happened? *You just thought us here?*"

Pyrope shrugged. "You said 'King' . . ."

"Then think us out of here!" I cried. "I just want to go home!"

Sounding like a growling Russian, the red man barked, "Classiify yoorself: Animal or Mineeral?"

Ignoring him, Jesse grabbed Pyrope. "You thought 'King' and … and that's how we got here?" he sputtered incredulously.

Pyrope shrugged helplessly.

Jesse called out to the ancient blue warrior on the gold throne. "Are you the King?" he inquired.

Impatiently, the tall red man raised his double-tipped sword and commanded imperiously, "SILENCE! You are in presence of—"

He stopped himself and remembered the trembling brown man kneeling before him. "For unlawful use of light," he proclaimed, "for hoarding, loss of clarity, and blasphemy—"

He stopped again, shrugged, and then casually tapped the brown man on the head with the white-hot scythed tip of his double sword.

There was a brilliant flash and explosion.

What was left of the brown man's light rushed into the red man's contorting crystal muscles and rippled out through the crowd, which moaned with pleasure.

Jesse grabbed my arm as we stared in shock.

Regarding the smoldering pile of brown dust at his feet, the red man sighed and finished his verdict: "Yoo are condemned to . . . daahst!"

Pointing the slicing edge of his incandescent sword toward the top of the white staircase, he fixed his eyes on us and announced, "Yoo are in presence of Sapphire King Beryl, 'Tha Bloo, Tha Rare, Tha True'—Ruler of House of Clarity in Land of Sedentia, Kingdom of Beryl!"

Then he bowed his head to the green Lady seated next to the King and added, "And Emerald Queen of Green."

The Queen of Green gave him a slight nod, and the red man lifted his proud chin in a smart salute.

Regarding Jesse and me with disdain, he announced condescendingly, "I am called Sapphire Red Prince, 'Tha Next, Tha Warrior, Tha True.' Classify yoorself!"

Had I heard right? She was emerald? And the King was sapphire? How much were they worth?

"Classify?" Jesse blurted. "I-I'm, uh . . . I'm human." The crowd gasped, and the Red Prince's faceted face tilted to the side as if he weren't sure of what he'd just heard.

Bounding down the white staircase, the small twisted man with the barely balancing cubes squealed in a squeaky Puerto Rican accent, "P-Pyrrite weel! I weel! I ham Court J-Jester. L-let meee! Let meee! L-let P-Pyrrite s-s-s-see!"

Snap!

Pyrite's red crystal leash had reached its end and vibrated angrily as his feet ran out from under him. He landed on his back with a splintering crash, and his left arm shattered, sending a couple of silver fingers skittering across the floor.

Standing beside the Green Queen, a cloudy orange man in a bright green and rust-colored crystal cape that squiggled with busy little yellow lines reached down and gave Pyrite's leash one more hard tug.

His chin yanking at his neck as though his collar were too small for him, he opened his large crystal lips, cleared his throat, and announced in a thick French accent, "I am bor-rn zee Or-range Sapphire Prince, 'Next to Zee Next Most Rar-re'! Yoo are een zee Court of Rools! Do not lie!"

"He's not lying!" I cried. "We are not lying. We just want to go home!"

The Red Prince pointed his horrible sword at me.

"Yoo are not Animal or Mineeral?" he demanded, and snorted contemptuously. "HA!" he barked. Then he barked again, "HA! HA!" sounding as if he were trying to spit up a hairball.

A rolling rumble of confusion filled the Royal Court. A purple man in a floppy black crystal hat threw up his hands in alarm, and a pink-and-white Lady with a blue-and-yellow tiara couldn't whisper fast enough to the crystal Lords and Ladies who craned their necks, waiting to see what the Red Prince would do next.

He didn't look as if he knew.

Pointing at Pyrope, Scheelite, and Torri, he changed the

subject. "They arr undress'd!" he declared. "Basalt Guards, cover them!"

Jesse raised his hand as if he were in school. "Where are we?" he asked. "Could you tell us—?"

"Attention, s'il vous plaît!" the Orange Prince interrupted with his chewy French accent. "Attention!"

He waited impatiently till the Court quieted down and two Basalt Guards draped Scheelite in a purple cape.

She blushed hot yellow, and Torri glowed red and actually made eyes at the Guard who was covering her.

"How har-rd ar-r zey?" the Orange Prince demanded, gargling his *R*'s and turning up his glowing nose as if he had just stepped in something that smelled awful. "What ees zere color-r?"

The Red Prince snorted disdainfully. "Why don't *you* make measure of them, small little brother?" he suggested smugly.

"Why don't yoo 'make measur-r' of zem, lava face?" the orange one whined, mimicking his muscular brother's Russian accent.

Showing multiple rows of red crystal teeth, the Red Prince smirked. "Iss Oranche Prince that is so small afraid?"

"Mind your huesss!" the Emerald Queen hissed menacingly, cutting off her bickering sons. "You are Princesss!"

Holding up her thin green claw, she pointed a long black fingernail at the balancing pile of Pyrite, who had just managed to get to his feet at the foot of the great staircase.

"Measure their facets, my little Pyrite!" she cooed, the tip of her pointy green tongue flicking between her teeth. "Measure the humans, my little fool."

"Oh, si, si! Tank yoo!" he squeaked, shivering in anticipation.

This was all Jesse's fault. He was playing one of his awful tricks on me. "Stop playing, Jesse!" I hissed at him. "This is a dream!" I insisted. "I want to wake up! I want to wake up!"

Regarding me curiously, Jesse shook his head. "This isn't a dream," he replied simply.

"It is a dream!" I cried. "This isn't real!"

Who were these people? Was Scheelite supposed to be me? I wasn't scared all the time like she was. I wasn't a flirt like Torri the Popsicle. I'd never be like that. And what about the Queen of Green, with her silver teeth that reminded me of my ugly braces? Were all of these creatures reflections of Jesse and me? What about the Red Prince and the Orange Prince and the Blue King? They didn't look anything like either of us! And the others! Who were the others? I couldn't wake up from this nightmare.

Pyrite's metallic feet clanged loudly on the floor as he limped up to me and smiled a mouthful of twisted crystals. Holding his miniature head-on-a-stick in front of his face, he tilted his own head, closed his roving red eye, and measured me with his green eye until it wandered off in search of the red one.

Addressing the Red Prince, Jesse explained, "We don't know how we got here, wherever 'here' is. If you could just tell us where—"

Pyrite couldn't get his mouth to close. His shaking hand minus three fingers was waving at me as if it wanted to fly away.

"Eet, eet m-m-moofs!" he stammered, staggering backward into Torri and getting all tangled up in his cubes.

A loud murmur rolled through the Court.

"It moves?" the Red Prince snorted loudly. "Of course it moves!" he scoffed. "They both move! Everyone sees this!"

"Eef, eef, eef. . ." Pyrite hiccupped, unable to get past his first word.

The Queen gave his leash a yank, and he spat out a tooth.

"If it p-please Your R-Royall R-Redness," Pyrite nervously continued, "and I ham afraid that eet w-will not please, or m-may n-not p-please," he percolated, and another jarring snap of his leash cost him a second tooth. "The th-thurface, eet, eet m-moofth!" he exclaimed now with a toothless lisp. "Een an' owth, owth an' een!" he cried.

The crowd gasped in alarm.

"Imbiceel!" the Orange Prince screeched impatiently, scrunching his fat face as his chin fought to get away from his neck. "Zen measure somesing zat doesn't moof!"

"Outh and een! Een and outh!" Pyrite desperately tried to explain to Torri as he pointed at me. "Eet m-moofth!"

Torri gave him a brilliant smile, and his metallic cubes instantly rearranged themselves and exploded with reflections of all her colors.

"Nithe r-rockth!" he stammered.

"Aah'll take that as uh gentleman's compliment, kind suh," she purred, coyly adjusting her new purple robe as Pyrite stared speechless.

"NON! Non, non, non!" the Orange Prince squawked, stamping his foot over and over like Jesse used to when I ignored him. "Not zee Popseecle!" he squealed, jabbing a fat crystal finger at Torri. "Touchez-la! Touchez-la!" he commanded, pointing at me.

Pyrite stabbed painfully at my arm, and his wandering mouth stretched into an *O* as the angles of his face rearranged themselves and his nose dropped an inch.

"Th-thoft!" he squeaked.

Crystals clicking to a crescendo, the Lords and Ladies started talking all at once, their lights ricocheting in staccato bursts.

Banging his huge blue ruler on the floor, the King struggled to get to his feet as Pyrite scrambled back up the staircase.

"The K-Keeng will thpeak! The K-Keeng will thpeak. Th-thpeak, thpeak—the K-Keeng will TH-THPEAK!" he lisped loudly.

A short round gray-and-brown rocklike man wearing oversized mica glasses appeared next to me. Blotchy horizontal lines of mica ran sideways throughout his body and reminded me of my dry skin in winter. Coming to attention, he stared straight ahead.

Jesse raised his hand *again*, "Before the King speaks," he politely requested, "we would like to know—"

Leaning across me, the short one introduced himself in a loud grating whisper, "Gneiss, Bailiff. Lower ya head, dummy!" he growled at Jesse like a gangster. "Da Rare, da True only speaks to da top of da bowed head."

I'd had enough of this. "Who are you and where are we?" I demanded angrily.

Lowering his own goody-goody head, Jesse hissed at me, "Maggie! Bow your head!"

"You bow *your* head!" I snapped.

The short, wide Bailiff sang out of the side of his mouth, "You're-not-bowin'-your-head."

So I bowed my head. Big deal.

I still peeked.

Kneeling before the King, a really skinny black-and-white stick of a servant held up a small green crystal box beneath the royal nose. With two long spidery fingers, the servant removed a pinch of gold dust, turned his face away, and offered it to the royal nostril.

It must have been that "snuff" stuff that people took a long time ago, because after King Bloo noisily inhaled it, his body rippled, his armor shook, and his straight golden rays became all squiggly.

With a lace handkerchief of crystals, the servant tried to catch up to the royal nose, but it was busy twitching, rearing back from something bigger—much bigger: a sneeze.

The Court waited.

The King concentrated.

Not a crystal clicked.

Not a clock ticked.

The King's finger shot straight up.

There was a collective gasp.

The royal nose carefully sniffed . . .

Tested an inhale . . .

Inhaled some more . . .

Then continued, relieved, till it could inhale no more.

The Court sighed in relief as the King shooed the servant away and searched for himself in a tall mica mirror that was being held for him by another black-and-white servant.

"ZERE ARE ROOLS!" King Bloo announced, sounding very German. "Rools for everysing! Rools of Value, Rools of Hardness, Rools of Color, Size, undt Clarity!"

With eyes closed, Gneiss the Bailiff nodded his rock head in rhythm, and swaying back and forth, silently mouthed the King's words with the rest of the Court.

"Rools of Use," the King continued, "Rools of Talking, Rools of Shtanding, Valking; Rools of Ownership, Behavior, undt Do!"

He sounded like Jesse with all his stupid rules about who could come into his room, or what was fair and whose turn it was.

Bowing their heads, the Court chanted in unison, "Behold the Descendant of Rulers—King Beryl, The Bloo, The Rare, The True!"

"Yoo will be rooled IN, undt rooled OUT!" the King commanded, and the entire Court clicked along as if keeping time.

"Rooled over, rooled under, against, undt for. Rooled goot undt bad, right undt wrong, rooled here, rooled zere, up und down, und everyvhere!"

"Da Blue man rules!" sang out Gneiss.

"EVERYSING HAS ROOLS!" declared King Bloo, his voice echoing into a solemn silence.

It reminded me of school.

Frantically chasing after King Bloo with another pinch of gold snuff, the servant's skinny fingers finally caught up to the King's other nostril.

Not a crystal budged as King Bloo loudly snuffed and sniffed it all up.

As the royal nose twitched, the wait became too much for the barely balancing Pyrite.

"I hate t-to be thee b-bearer of bad t-tidingth, Your Royal Rare," he sputtered, his lisp getting even worse. "But they eeth th-thoft an' their out-thide eeth m-moofing', an' th-thee others were undreth'd, an' there eeth no r-rool for——"

"EVERYSING HAS ROOLS!" the King barked, then fell into a pout. "Else I refuse to discuss viz it! Zat is . . . a . . . ah . . . aahh . . . aaaahhhh—"

Immediately ducking their heads, the entire crystal court quickly covered their ears and squeezed their eyes shut as the King did battle with the Sneeze.

And lost.

"Aaaahhh, aaahh—CHOOOOO!"

A great wind blew. Crystal hats, hair, capes, and canes flew through the air. The pink-and-white Lady's tiara hit the Orange Prince in the face, and two crystal pet dogs blew past, leaving a trail of light that was followed by a great chorus of voices chanting, "Metabless You! Metabless You! METABLESS YOU!"

Nearly choking on the end of his declaration, the King sputtered, "A . . . a . . . R-Roool!" then collapsed into a cough.

Snaking down the silvery stairs, the Emerald Queen slid between her red and orange sons. "Come, my little afterthoughtsss," she hissed.

Jesse cleared his throat. "But, but Your Honor," he called up to the King. "I mean, Your Bloo, Your, uh, Rareness. We have no idea of how we got here! One minute we were—"

King Bloo's right hand shot straight up; he'd forgotten his favorite rule.

"Undt if zere is a rool zat somesing CANNOT be talked about," he pronounced, ". . . ZEN IT VON'T BE TALKED ABOUT!"

Teetering uncertainly, he slumped back into his throne, exhausted.

"This is ridiculous!" I blurted. "You are rocks! Stupid rocks! We don't have to—"

"We only want to know what we're doing here!" Jesse interrupted, still trying to be reasonable.

"I don't care what I'm doing here!" I yelled angrily. "I want to go home!"

A hush fell over the Court as the Emerald Queen slithered toward us.

"Dis is not good," Gneiss muttered, nervously shaking his head, "Dis is not . . . good."

A slice of a smile slowly slid across her green face, and her thin purple tongue darted from between her rows of pointy silver teeth.

"Your s-s-surface, it moves-s?" she purred to Jesse.

"Yes," explained Jesse, "because we breathe."

A thin, jagged yellow line of light rippled through her body and she shuddered. "You 'breathe'?" she inquired, as if she didn't know the meaning of the word.

Jesse nodded. "Air," he explained to the hovering Queen, who looked like a snake about to strike. "We breathe air: in and out."

A wave of gasps and crystal clicks chased a rolling pulse of light as it washed through the crowd.

The Queen's laugh sounded like breaking glass and her yellowy lines did a little jig. "You breathe aaiirrr?" she asked incredulously, her body curving into a question mark.

"Everything breathes," I snapped.

Snorting, the Red Prince proudly raised his chin and

sword and addressed the ceiling. "We have not to breathe. We radiate," he proclaimed pompously.

Turning to me, Gneiss sarcastically imitated the Red Prince. "We radiate!" he whispered, only to turn back and discover the black tip of the Queen's long green finger pulsing at the end of his nose.

"You were ssaying?" she hissed.

"Nothin'!" blurted Gneiss, breaking out into a serious mica rash. "I wasn't sayin' nothin'!"

The Orange Prince was clearly feeling left out.

"Une question!" he announced importantly, his chin tugging impatiently at his neck. "Wher-re, and fr-rom which place, are yoo fr-rom?" he demanded with a lot of phlegmy *R*'s.

"Earth," Jesse answered obligingly. "In the air, up on top of the earth."

That set off another surge of light undulating through the crystal crowd and an even louder rumble of confusion.

Smirking at such obvious stupidity, the Orange Prince corrected Jesse. "Yoo mean under, below," he insisted, "from zee hell zat ees zee Land of Air."

"No. Not below, on top, above," Jesse patiently explained obviously unaware that these people couldn't understand a word of what he was saying. "You know, up? Outside? Where there are people, plants, and animals?"

"NEIN! Yoo cannot be from za Air!" King Bloo sputtered, turning a bit purple.

Leaning into Jesse, Gneiss whispered, "I don' tink you wanna go to dat particular place," he suggested tactfully.

I couldn't believe that these people were so dense!

"Well, we are from 'za Air,' okay?" I yelled at the King impatiently. "We fell into a hole, okay? A dark hole where there was no light. My brother turned on his flashlight, and suddenly there was light going everywhere, all at once!" I pointed to Torri, Pyrope, and Scheelite, who were staring at me, petrified, "Then they came alive. Ask them!"

Vibrating with angry sparks of light, the crowd jostled each other, and the pink-and-white Lady fainted in a heap of crystals.

A chunky yellow couple began laughing so hysterically that they had to sit down on the blue floor.

Smacking me on the head, Pyrite peevishly proclaimed, "Yoo cannot b-bee thee Humanth! What eeth there c-cannot c-come here!" he declared, smacking me again. "Thee d-down below eeth filled w-weeth thee Humanth," he lisped, spitting sprays of light. "They are c-cold and hard weethout thee l-light, thtuck een b-boxeth of wood and thtone or crushed f-forever een thee Land of F-Fotheels. What eeth there c-cannnot c-come here!" he claimed, smacking me a third time with a mischievous sparkle in his red eye. "That eeth thee Rool!"

"Then I guess someone broke your silly rules!" I barked, threatening to smack him back.

That shut everyone up.

Gneiss leaned as far away from the Queen as he could and cleared his throat. "She gotta point, Ya Rareness," he rasped.

King Bloo stared at Gneiss in confusion.

"Undt who are you?" he demanded.

Gneiss bowed his head. The top of his noggin was covered with mica hives.

"Name's Granular Gneiss. Local S.P.C.R.," he announced officially.

The King didn't have a clue what 'Local S.P.C.R.' meant.

"Da Society for da Prevention of Cruelty tuh Rocks," Gneiss nervously reminded the King, expecting the Queen's wrath to descend on him at any second.

"Who brought zem here?" King Bloo finally thundered, his body crackling with light.

"Hoo-hoo brought them here? Hoo-hoo brought them here?" parroted Pyrite, flickering furiously in the King's reflected light. "Hoo-hoo brought th-tha Humanth oneth h-heerr?"

"Who brrought who where?" the Orange Prince cried in confusion, his chin continuing its tug of war with his neck.

With an angry flash of yellow, the Green Queen swatted him upside his orange head.

"I think it was I, Your Bloo," Pyrope's voice softly echoed.

Nobody moved.

"Who speaks?" King Bloo demanded.

Stepping forward, Pyrope raised his hand and bowed his head.

"I am named Pyrope, Your Bloo," he nervously replied. "I think I was the one who brought them here."

"You 'think' this?" growled the Red Prince disdainfully.

"Eesn't zat what he has jus' said?" The Orange Prince pecked at his red brother and then repeated it for him: "Zee Pyrope person said he 'sinks'!"

"Who vas za vun zat named you za 'Pyr-rope,' common crystal?" demanded the King.

Pyrope raised his head and pointed at Jesse. "The Human," he said, "when he created me."

That caused a really big commotion. Gneiss's mouth hung open in surprise, and the crystal Lords and Ladies spewed their light in alarm. The two yellow chunky ones with the green crystal spikes rolled on the floor, laughing so hard that their light crackled out of control.

"I didn't create anything!" Jesse yelled over the noise.

"He just turned on his flashlight!" I cried. "What can't you understand?"

"What'd he toin on?" Gniess anxiously asked me under his breath.

Sneering, the Red Prince barked at Pyrope, "You think they create you? And you think you bring Huminns to here from Sedentian Plains?"

Pyrope shrugged. "I, I don't know how," he replied. "They appeared in a storm of light. Then others came to be, and we were surrounded by hordes of unfinished creatures demanding light. They attacked us, and the Human said the word *King*, and before I knew what happened—"

"YOU MOVE THEM?" the Red Prince interrupted in shock. "You move them with yoor *mind*?"

Chaos.

You'd think all these crystal people were about to be dug up.

Gneiss put a scaly hand on my arm. "Don't worry. I got dis," he reassured me.

The Orange Prince's chin circled his face, looking for a place to land. "Don' bee very r-ridiculous!" he sniffed incredulously. "Zere ees nossing on zee Plains Sedentienne. Eet is void. Eeet is empty."

"He move zem, idiot!" the Red Prince bellowed, his red crystals boiling with light and his booming voice crashing off the walls. "It is against law for a common crystal to move—anything! Anywhere!" he declared angrily.

Raising his hand again, Pyrope respectfully explained, "I didn't know I was moving anyone, or, or doing anything. I mean, I didn't mean to. I thought—"

"Zee common crystal eez lying!" the Orange Prince stated flatly. "I ham positeef!" he bragged, enjoying the sound of his own voice. "He ees not telling zee whole tr-rooss; eet ees impossible to moof zem from zee Plains Sedentienne because zere ees no light on zee Plains Sedentienne! Of zis we are certain!" He paused for effect, his chin vibrating intensely. "It ees dark and wizzout illoomination on zee Plains Sedentienne! Zere ees nothing zere!"

Gneiss nodded quickly, and there was a great click and clack of agreement, as the Court pounced on the comfort of a known fact.

"Am *I* nothing? Am I without light?" Scheelite's fragile voice pierced the din. "Are all those we left in Sedentia 'nothing'?" she demanded of the Orange Prince, surprising herself by her outburst, her trembling yellow crystals frightened white. "And what is a 'King'? What is a 'Prince'?" she asked emphatically.

In a buzzing briar patch of light, the Royal Court waited for the Orange Prince to respond to this preposterous demand from a common crystal, but he could only stand there stunned, his mouth opening and closing with fizzles of orange light leaking out.

Abruptly extending one of his surging blades from its hilt, the Red Prince held the white-hot tip inches from my face. "Crush these Humans! SEND THEM TO FOSSILIA!" he proclaimed.

The crowd roared.

"No!" cried Pyrope, protectively putting his arm around Scheelite. "Please!"

Holding up both hands in objection, Gneiss raised his voice. "Due process . . . dere's gotta be due process," he insisted.

Hopping from one metallic foot to the other, Pyrite danced with excitement. "C-c-crush them! C-crushh them! Thend them to F-fothillia!"

"We can explain!" Jesse protested, turning to me for help.

Regally marching across the room, the Orange Prince stopped before Scheelite, made a grand gesture with his hand and chin, and then bowed very low before her.

"I—I, MOI—ma chère," the Orange Prince announced gallantly, with another flourish of his bejeweled hand, "I ham a Pr-reence!"

King Bloo and the Royal Court stared in shock at the Orange Prince bowing to a commoner.

The Green Queen shook her head and covered her eyes as a singular sigh split the silence, and Scheelite's blushing light rolled up her yellow face.

Gneiss raised a stony finger and cleared his throat. "Ya Bloo? If I may? Dere ain't a lot of, ahhh, precedent in dis, uh, particular situation."

Purring, the Green Queen whispered at my ear, "I like your shiny teeth. Are we related?"

I could see the reflection of my braces in her yellow eyes.

"They're braces, and no, we are not," I answered, trying to keep my voice from trembling.

A scary smile slithered across her face. "You'd be s-s-surprised," she cooed. "You'd be very s-surprised!" Then she leaned in even closer. "You turned on *what* light and created *whom*?"

My heart was racing, but I wasn't going to let her know I was scared. I turned away and glimpsed Jesse hiding his flashlight in his pocket.

"You don't want me to turn yel-l-low, do you?" she crooned softly.

Pyrite's head jerked up and down in eager anticipation.

"They made laaght!" Torri blurted.

Stepping forward, she put her rainbow arm around

Scheelite's trembling shoulders and proudly drawled. "And in that laaght we became sistuhs! We found each othuh!"

The Court erupted in a dither. "They made what?" "Found who?" "Whose sister?"

Pivoting to Torri, the Green Queen hissed, "What did you s-s-say?"

Torri sighed and repeated herself as if to a three-year-old, "Aahh said, they made LAAGHT, and we became SISTUHS!"

In that moment, I liked Torri. She was my kind of girl. She wasn't about to let some green queen scare her.

"Do we have tuh spell it out for yuh?" she continued passionately. "We saw laaght. We saw each othuh. We saw ouahselves!"

This was too much for the crystal Court.

King Bloo dropped his ruler, which clattered down the stairs as his subjects started booing Torri and throwing handbags and other crystal objects.

Laughing derisively, the Red Prince challenged Torri. "How?" he growled. "How is ziss?"

The Orange Prince had the answer. "Écoutez, imbecile!" he screeched impatiently at his brother. "Listen wiz yoor ears, not yoor muscles! Zey jus' tell you how; zey made light. Zat ees how zey moofed," he concluded with a couple of decisive jerks of his chin.

THE KINGDOM OF BERYL

"No one makes light!" barked the Red Prince.

A cacophony of confusion filled the Court.

"SILENCE!" screeched the Emerald Queen, convulsing in a spasm of yellow flashes.

The furor grew.

"NEIN!" King Bloo bellowed, "Zis cannnot be! It will not be!"

Viciously scratching at the mica rash on the top of his head, Gneiss yelled into my ear, "Dis ain't good. Dis is definitely, definitely not good!"

A painfully high whine pierced the room.

Trying to block out the pain, I grabbed my ears as a bone-rattling *CRAAACK* shook the entire building.

The entire Court immediately fell to their knees, closed their eyes, and bowed their heads as two huge doors at the end of the hall were swallowed up in a blinding light.

Belief

Mom loved to skate.

At first ice she'd bundle us up and we'd hike to Fuller's pond, where we had to take a running jump over the new ice that was too thin to skate on at the watery edge.

Laughing with delight, Mom would go first. She'd leap, and the rubbery black ice would bubble and bow beneath her flying skates as spider-thin cracks chased after her flashing blades with deep snapping groans.

Then she was safe, spinning into an I-told-you-so pose, her arms held out to us, and her smile steaming in the cold air.

Jesse would then whoop and holler and run on his dull double-bladers across the paper-thin ice to Mom's waiting arms.

I always knew that my foot would go through.

Thousands of tiny exploding rainbows converged in the white brilliance.

Squinting, I could barely make out a tall shape floating in the blinding light. It looked like a robe of glittering diamonds billowing about a blazing staff.

It was a man—an impossibly thin and very tall glistening man with a long sparkling beard.

I grabbed Jesse. "Are those d-diamonds?" I gasped. "Is he all diamonds?"

Suddenly the white light evaporated and the shrill sound stopped.

Everything went still.

Slowly opening his mouth, the old man pointed a thin sparkling finger at us.

"Youa stand ina tha presence offa The Holy Cleara, Knower offa All Things Lighta," he declared. He sounded like an ancient Italian vampire, and his hoarse voice seemed to come from all around us.

Chanting as one, the entire Royal Court rocked back and forth on their feet, chanting, "Metabless the Holy Clear Knower of All Things Light!"

His finger drifted from one brilliant diamond to another, touching them as if he were pointing out a sacred map.

"Lighta issa eternal! Lighta has allaways beena!" he chanted grimly in his ancient voice. "Lighta will allaways beea; ita gives us whata we seea, whata we knowa. It destr-roys the dar-rka, r-reveals beauty, ugliness, whata issa talla, shor-rta, gooda, bada, uppa, downa, lefta and r-righta; closa, fara, r-richa and poor-ra . . ."

Their heads bowed, the Royal Court raised their hands to the crystal ceiling and echoed, "RICHER AND POORER . . ."

Gneiss sang out loudly, "Say da truth! Speak da woids!"

Surrounded by his aura of shimmering light, the old man sang, "Wea glitter toa glor-rify tha lighta offa our Lor-rda Metamor-rphos, hallowed be thy Nayma!"

The Lords and Ladies lifted their voices: "Metabless Metamorphos, hallowed be Thy Name!"

"His Lighta lets us see whata issa!" he rasped. "Forra alla that ISSA, issa whata we seea. And alla we seeah issa ALLA that ISSA!"

"All That IS!" the Royal Court replied.

"And alla that ISSA, ISSA all thata we KNOWA!" he declared.

"All We Know!" they roared.

Stopping abruptly, he raised his thin sparkling arms before the hushed Court and, trembling, turned to Jesse and me.

"Youa!" he wheezed in a harsh whisper. "Youa come from tha Outsida, tha Nothing." His eyes were white with light. "Tha Hell Belowa; tha Land offa Air-ra. Your poisoned waters rise uppa froma your-ra dark and airy depthsa, and pollootta, cor-roda, an' destr-roya!" he proclaimed solemnly.

"Pollute. Corrode. Destroy!" repeated the Royal Court.

"Youa bury yourselves ina wooda and stona boxes, condemned toa softeness and decaya, sur-rounded bya tha tweesting r-rootsa," he accused darkly. "You who reacha ina vain for-ra tha glorious Lighta of Metamorphia, our-ra Heaven, our-ra Core."

Eyes tightly shut, and swaying back and forth on his heels, the Orange Prince sang out above everyone else, "Holeee, Holeee!!"

"YOU AR-RA NOTTA!" the Holy Clear declared, pointing at Jesse and me. "And, you who 'Ar-ra Notta' ar-ra condemned to tha dar-rkness of Fossiliia to be cruhshed forever inna tha Landa offa Fossiils!"

Caught completely by surprise and the possibility of a ruling, King Bloo leapt to his feet. "SO BE IT!" he proclaimed, nearly falling over.

"Th-tho b-be eet!" parroted Pyrite in his clippy lisp.

The Orange Prince waved a hand in protest as he struggled to clear his throat. "Pardon, s'il vous plaît. Eef I may," he requested airily, grabbing his twitching neck with his hand and giving a reassuring wink to Scheelite. "Perhaps zere ees an uzzer way, an alter-rnateef—"

"Nyett!" interrupted the Red Prince. "So be it!" he declared, raising his two-bladed sword high above his head. "They will be crushed forever in Llannd of Fossiils!"

I couldn't believe it. They were going to crush us?

"Then why aren't we dead?" I cried indignantly. "Why aren't we buried in wood, or stone?" I wanted to crush every one of them. "Because I don't know why me and my brother are down here, or 'up' here, or wherever 'here' is," I yelled. "But we are definitely not dead! We are alive, and we are from the 'Land of Air,' which is not a 'hell'! It is a heaven and it is filled with light! What do you say to that?" I threatened, trembling with anger.

The entire Court stared at me with their crystal mouths hanging open.

Gneiss's grating voice eventually split the silence. "Dat's a good question," he acknowledged, nodding his head.

That unleashed a mighty clamor.

Leaping to his feet, King Bloo re-attacked the floor with his ruler, nearly crushing Pyrite, who flew up with a sharp squeak, landed on his butt, and bounced down the stairs, chipping a few cubes in the process.

"Thee K-Keeng weel th-thpeak!" he spluttered. "Thee K-Keeng weel th-thpeak!"

Then something strange happened.

A bone-chilling moan chased a large dark shadow that washed through the entire place.

"Uh oh . . ." muttered Gneiss.

Jesse reached for my hand as an eerie silence descended.

King Bloo's face went slack, and the Green Queen straightened like a needle on her spine.

Clear crystals became opaque as the pulsing cores within the creatures' bodies dimmed.

The only sound was the faint clicking of shivering crystals brushing together as though a cold wind had blown through them.

Then the darkness left as quickly as it had come.

Everybody and everything reignited with light. Gneiss sighed out loud as the bright clinking of crystals replaced the dry rattle of a moment ago, and the room filled with sighs of relief, even though a few of the Ladies had fainted dead away.

"What was that?" Jesse blurted.

"What was what?" Gneiss answered too quickly.

"It just got darker," Pyrope replied.

"Blasphameea!" screeched the Holy Clear, pointing a trembling diamond finger at Pyrope.

The Court ooohed in fear.

"It did! It got darker," I argued. "I saw it. We all saw it!"

Eyes raging, the Holy Clear cried out, "You tayka tha Lord's nayma inna vain. It issa tha 'TOOA and FR-ROA.' It is only tha 'Tooa and Fr-roa'!"

Two Guards helped him onto his knees, and he raised his skinny sparkling arms high above his head. "Kneel beefore tha r-rhythm offa tha Lighta. Beholda tha Glory of—"

"Our light is dying," a soft, very clear woman's voice interrupted him.

The words hung over the stunned crowd.

"We've just seen it," insisted the voice. "Our light is dying!"

A rustle of apprehension filled the room as a beautiful young Lady stepped gracefully from the crowd.

Surrounded by an aura of violet light, her lovely gown of purple crystals softly glowed as her radiance undulated up to clear pink crystals and pale violet hair that was crowned with a sparkling tiara.

A single Basalt Guard attended her as she stopped and bowed to the King.

King Bloo seemed to melt in front of her.

She smiled at the Emerald Queen, who looked away from her with a yellow shiver.

Addressing the royal gathering, the beautiful violet Lady spoke in a firm, quiet voice. "Our light is dying. Why are we forbidden to speak those words?"

Gneiss shook his head in resignation.

Torri inhaled loudly. "Oh maaah!" she blurted, nervously examining her own crystals for lost light.

"Blasphameea!" the Holy Clear wheezed again as the two Basalt Guards helped him back onto his feet.

The beautiful Lady acknowledged him. "Look at you. Look at us!" she implored. "The Human is right, and very much alive. It *is* getting darker."

The Royal Court erupted in a panic of angry voices.

Avoiding a warning glare from the Green Queen, King Bloo chanced a glance toward the Holy Clear, who was staring at the beautiful Lady as if she were poisonous.

"This issa heresy!" the Holy Clear lashed out in horror. "You arra sinning, Princhessa Amitheessta!"

Ignoring his warning, Princess Amethyst addressed the Royal Court. "Why can't we say what we see when we can all see it?"

They stared at her in mute fear.

Gneiss held his palms up and shrugged a *what're-ya-gonna-do?* to the Princess as her personal Basalt Guard followed her over to Pyrope, whose garnets blushed when she smiled at him.

"And they have 'moved,'" she continued, gently placing her violet hand on Pyrope's glowing arm and turning to the Royal Court. "How is that? How is it that the Pyrope here moved them? The good Pyrope, who is known to avert evil thoughts and foretell misfortunes?"

She curtsied to Torri and Scheelite. "The good Pyrope says the beautiful Scheelite, keeper of the spirit of strength, and the equally beautiful Tourmaline, gemstone of love and friendship, were created by the light of the Humans. Who will speak to the 'why' of them?"

"You?" the Red Prince sneered.

Banging his ruler, King Bloo demanded, "Who will speak to za 'why' of Zem? Zere must be a rool!" he announced, stealing a peek at the Emerald Queen, who was turning even more yellow at his defense of their daughter.

"Good," remarked Gneiss sarcastically. "We need more rules."

The Orange Prince's bejeweled finger stabbed at the air. "Zee why!" he repeated, as if it were his own edict. "C'est le moment for une rool!" he pointed emphatically with his chin, trying to impress Scheelite and everybody else with his wisdom and leadership.

"Issa imposseeble!" sputtered the Holy Clear.

"ZISS IS IMPOSSIBLE!" King Bloo echoed, instantly changing his mind.

"Porquoi?" the Orange Prince insisted dramatically, and then repeated his question to Scheelite, "Pourquoi pourquoi?" as if he were blowing her kisses. "POURQUOI? Why?" he asked with vain sincerity. "I haf always honored zee question 'why?' Eet ees a good—"

An olive-green claw latched possessively onto the Orange Prince's arm as a sickly Lady, with dull spikes of olive light pulsing weakly at her thin joints, insinuated herself and her muddy brown cape between the Orange Prince and Scheelite.

"Perhaps Princess Amethyst asks too difficult a question at too difficult a time," she whined in a high nasal voice down a very long nose. "Who are *we* to question the 'why?'" she asked, fixing Scheelite with a cold smile, "when our Holy Clear reminds us that there are some things that are *beyond* our knowing?"

"Why can't we speak of that which we *don't* know?" asked a tall, pale blue Lady who stepped from the crowd with two slinky Ladies of black obsidian following her. "Can you deny that the Humans exist, Lady Hiddenite?"

"Eet ees imposeeble! I cannot!" the Orange Prince gushed at Scheelite, who immediately blushed into the floor.

Lady Hiddenite looked as if she were having a bad gas attack.

Princess Amethyst bowed to the pale blue Lady. "Thank you, Princess Topaz, protector against evil and ill health, and the Obsidian Twins who enhance intuition."

Snorting disdainfully, the Red Prince smirked. "Ha! Da Vibrayshun Sisters!"

The Royal Court snickered.

"Amethist Princess should spik about what she knows," he suggested derisively.

Admonishing Princess Amethyst, the Holy Clear raised a thin hand, "You arra trespassing into-a sin, Princhessa Amitheesta. You arra forgetting—"

"You do best to stick to that what you do best, leetle seester," the Red Prince interrupted with a rotten red smile. "Peddle piety, humility, and sobriety," he sneered.

Princess Amethyst returned the compliment with an even smile. "What I do best, my suffering brother, is something you may never know."

"Hah!" guffawed the Red Prince. "Then perhaps you should join tha priesthood of tha Holy Clear," he replied, and the Lords and Ladies laughed, relieved at the distraction.

"Lighta does notta DIE!" the Holy Clear declared vehemently. "Lighta issa FOREVER!"

"FOREVER!" chimed the entire Court.

I couldn't take any more of this stupidity.

"My brother created your light!" I yelled at these crystal idiots. "It was completely dark when we—"

"Holda!" the Holy Clear blazed, instantly blinding me with a blast of light from his diamond finger. "You will nota speaka. You arra condemned to tha Land ofa Fossilia!"

"Objection!" Gneiss called out with a raised finger.

"Why?" I shot back at the Holy Clear's brilliant glare. "Why do we have to go to this, this 'Fossilia'? We didn't do anything!"

"Please!" Jesse interrupted. "Everything gets dark," he begged. "Light does go away, but it comes back. It always comes back."

"It goes away?" panicked Gneiss.

"Jesse!" I hissed, grabbing his arm. "They don't believe that!"

"That's right," he insisted, "because they don't *know*."

"Light goes away never!" the Red Prince scoffed. "It cannot go away. Ever! Light makes since before memory. This is To and Fro only. So is written, so is done."

Gneiss nodded in agreement. "So it is written."

"But it does go away," Jesse barged on, sounding like our mother. "And day follows night, just as spring follows winter—"

"Silenceea!" screeched the Holy Clear.

"Listen to him!" Princess Amethyst pleaded. "Listen to what the Human says!"

Grabbing the Princess by the arm, the Holy Clear waved his crystal staff at the Guards as he dragged her toward us. "Basalta Guardsa!" he commanded, while the crowd watched, stunned.

The King jumped to his feet in defense of his daughter, then sat back down before the Queen's punishing gaze.

Two of the Basalt Guards seized Princess Amethyst's personal Guard and marched him over as well.

Pyrope ran to the Princess's rescue, and a third Guard knocked him down as Scheelite rushed to his side.

The Court erupted in confusion.

"Spreeng, weenter, spreeng weenter?" the Orange Prince sputtered, shaking his head. "W-what ees zees 'spreeng-weenter'?"

Yelling over the surrounding circle of Basalt Guards, Jesse tried to explain, "Spring comes *after* winter, after the dark. My mother always says it's darkest just before the dawn!"

"Sach dreevel iss this!" the Red Prince snarled.

I yanked Jesse's flashlight from his pocket.

"Here! Here is your stupid light!" I shouted. "And it hasn't always been! It wasn't even here an hour ago!"

"Don't!" Jesse yelped fearfully, reaching to take it back from me.

"Jesse, they're here because of the flashlight!" I hissed.

"But batteries die!" he insisted, grabbing my arm. "There has to be another reason …"

"An 'hour-a-go'? What's an hour-a-go?" Gneiss hollered.

"It's the way we keep time!" I cried, trying to get my finger on the button as Jesse's nails dug into my skin.

"You keep time?" inquired Gneiss, amazed. "Where do you keep it?"

Finally managing to push the button, I screamed, "Blaspheme this!"

The white beam ricocheted off the ceiling, instantly shattering into a minor light storm, and the Royal Court screamed in panic.

The Emerald Queen turned bright green and started to vibrate as the amazed Red Prince watched his crystal muscles twist and swell with boiling explosions of red light.

Princess Amethyst's deep violet crystals crackled clear in the crashing light and Pyrite, tickled by his cubes' sizzling surfaces, giggled hysterically and vibrated so violently that he lost his balance and fell onto his back, fracturing a couple of corners.

"ISSA FALSA LIGHTA! FALSA TROOTHA!" the Holy Clear shrieked, his body exploding in the dazzling light as his flashing eyes locked on the flashlight.

"It's light from batteries!" Jesse yelled, trying to pry my finger off the button.

Gneiss stared wide-eyed at the mini-explosions of light erupting from his surface. "I've . . . I've got 'spahkle!'" he exclaimed excitedly.

The Queen pulled the Red Prince into a wide-eyed whisper, jabbing her incandescent finger at Jesse's flashlight as the Holy Clear screamed.

"SIEZA THEMA! CRUSHA THEMA! STONA THEM ATTA ONCE!"

King Bloo, spewing streams of golden light, rose from his throne, looking taller, bluer, and younger, then met Princess Amethyst's pleading eyes and slowly lowered his head in disgrace amid the blasting beams.

Bombarded by brilliant streaks ricocheting throughout his body, the Orange Prince tried to reach over the circle of Basalt Guards for Scheelite, but he couldn't control his body. The light caromed through him so violently that he found himself staggering backwards, away from the circle.

"Pyrope, help!" Jesse yelled fearfully as Pyrope stood stunned by the spikes and sprays of red light shooting off his entire body.

The light storm kept getting louder and brighter.

"Tayka them! Crusha them! Nowa!" the Holy Clear commanded, pushing Princess Amethyst and her personal Guard into the circle of Basalt Guards.

"But there is more; there is so much more!" Princess Amethyst pleaded.

"Hold on! Hold on!" Gneiss hollered, wildly waving his blistering arms about. "He said 'dem'! I'm not 'dem'!"

Torri fainted at his feet.

Making another try amid the blazing beams, the Orange Prince got two fingers on Scheelite's arm. "Here, chérie, here! Take zee hand!" he implored. "Take zee hand!" But he was yanked away by the Red Prince, who muscled his deforming body between the Basalt Guards and tore my hand with the flashlight from Jesse's grasp.

"No! Please! Let us go home!" I cried hysterically. The skin on my hand felt as if it were burning from the Red Prince's splintering claw, but I refused to let go of the flashlight.

"Pyrope, you gotta do something!" Jesse screamed.

The crashing beams were becoming so bright that colors were disappearing and everything was turning white. The Red Prince twisted my arm, and the flashlight's beam hit him in the eye.

I could barely see him in the exploding flashes. He howled and jerked about as he held on to me. His crystal muscles popped and bulged, and his body twisted even more grotesquely as his face shattered into a web of fracturing facets.

I couldn't see!

I could feel Jesse trying to tear my burning hand from the Red Prince's grasp.

"No!" I screamed and pulled as hard as I could.

Pain shot like lightning through my shoulder and exploded into my head.

I could feel Jesse's fingers grabbing for the flashlight, and the last thing I heard was his voice screaming, "PYROPE!"

FOSSILIA

Jesse was my slave.

Whenever I told him that something was a "big secret" and that it was just between the two of us and he couldn't tell anyone, especially Mommy and Daddy, he would do anything I asked.

If I wanted to get rid of him, I'd send him on a "mission" in search of treasure. When he came back, I'd ask him a lot of questions that I knew he wouldn't be able to answer and then send him off on another "mission."

I told him there was a monster under my bed, and that's how I kept him out of my room.

Jesse believed anything and everything I told him, until one night when he wouldn't stop bothering me.

I had a friend sleeping over, and I told him that if he didn't leave us alone he would never, ever be able to believe in anything again, ever.

He looked at me with a strange expression, and then asked, "Even you?"

A universe, a cosmos of a zillion twinkling lights exploded in a dark void around us, and I prayed that I was still dreaming.

Jesse and I stood in an island of light created by the pulsing glow coming from Princess Amethyst, her Basalt Guard, Pyrope, Scheelite, Gneiss, and Torri, who were staring out at a world of dark silhouettes that loomed above us.

Some looked like dark cutouts of giant trees, twisted limbs, and leafless branches; others were great angular shapes that rose up and towered over us.

We were in a black-and-gray world of shadows—huge shadows going in every direction till they disappeared into an inky darkness pricked with countless sparkling lights resembling the stars of a nebula.

"What happened?" whispered Gneiss shakily. "Where are we?"

"This is FosSSIILLIAA," the Basalt Guard softly grunted in a guttural burst, like one of those Japanese ninjas who sound as if they're constantly trying to clear their throats. "The Land of FOSSILS!" he announced, then pointed to the twinkling lights. "And the reflected lights of MY-caah!"

"Fahssilia?" Torri asked anxiously, her neon colors flashing up and down. She reminded me of an out-of-control traffic light. "How'd we get heah?"

Pyrope shrugged. "Fossilia was the only place I heard," he replied hesitantly. "I didn't know what else to do."

"So ya moved us?" Gneiss fumed. "To Fossilia?" he growled incredulously, scratching at a glowing rash that was nearly covering his entire body. "Sure, why not? Dat's a terrific idea! Let's all move to da Land of Fossils and get crushed!" he wailed, before sticking his angry face into Pyrope's and squealing, "Ya got rocks in ya head?"

"There wasn't a lot of choice," Scheelite suggested timidly. "It was either that or—"

"Dis is where ya get crushed, Miss Yelluh!" Gneiss hollered angrily, waving his short arms about. "Dere's nuttin' here! It's da end of da line—kaput, finished, ovah! We may as well jus' lie down and wait to get flattened!" he yelled and plopped down in a puff of dust.

Scheelite started to cry.

"Ahh wuhd luv tuh laah down!" Torri sighed, leaning on the Basalt Guard, who was doing his best not to stare at her pulsing colors.

"It was actually the safest place," offered the Princess.

Gneiss snorted sarcastically. "Oh, really? Dat's good, 'cause I feel really safe—really, really safe!"

"How do you do that?" I demanded of Pyrope. "How do you move us around underground—through solid rock?"

Like a cat with a hairball stuck in its throat, the Basalt Guard proclaimed, "It's a Royal SECRET. Only they remember how."

"Oh, really?" I asked this basalt bozo. "If it's such a 'royal secret,' how did Pyrope move us? Twice?"

Nobody had an answer for that one.

Princess Amethyst finally spoke up. "It has to do with the light," she explained.

"What does moving have to do with light?" Jesse interrupted, confused.

"We believe," she continued, "that back before memory, when the Great Flash occurred and light was created by Metamorphos—God of Light and Wizard of Iz—the light went everywhere at the same time and gave us the knowledge that we are a part of everything, and everything is a part of us."

"There's a wizard?" Jesse asked, lighting up at the mention of the word.

"Yeah," I snorted, "in Oz."

Gneiss snorted as well. "Hah, Metamorphos?" he said, smirking. "Da Wizard of Iz, who supposedly lives beyond da Land of Magma?"

Pyrope began muttering, "Land of Magma, Land of Magma—"

Gneiss nearly jumped down his throat. "Don't! Don't even say it! Don't even tink about it!"

"Master Gneiss says 'supposedly,'" replied the Princess,

"because, according to legend, only the ancestors of King Bloo have ever actually been there. It is believed—"

"So nobody knows this for sure?" I interrupted, "They just believe? Of course. You aren't even real. Does anybody here know anything at all?" I asked angrily.

Then Jesse started talking about how, in his book *Science Wonder Stories*, there's no space for people to move physically so they have to move with their minds. Jesse could be really dense sometimes.

"That's a comic book, dummy!" I reminded him.

Sticking out his chin the way he did when he was wrong, Jesse yelped, "Hey, Maggot, I'm not the one who turned on the flashlight! Maybe if you can think it, it can be real and you can move into another time, or dimension."

"I don't care about another time or dimension!" I snapped and turned to the Princess. "I just want to go home to my mom and my dad, my room, and my bed! Why can't I just 'move' home?"

"I'm sure you do want to go home," she said softly, nodding her head, "but that's something only Metamorphos, the Wizard of Iz, knows. It is believed that moving happens when you know the source of light and the truth of yourself."

She said this as if she were explaining why it was important to put out cookies for Santa Claus on Christmas Eve. I didn't have a clue what she was talking about.

"We have the source of light! We have the flashlight!" I reminded the Princess.

The Princess went on, explaining that Pyrope was able to move us to Fossilia because he has the 'knowing' of Fossilia. She then said that earth, all that is earth, all that is underground, is a part of Pyrope, and that he is a part of it. "He has no knowing of the Land of Air because he has never seen or experienced it."

"But air is a part of him. There's air down here," Jesse pointed out. "Maggie and me are breathing. Aren't ground and air all part of the same thing?"

The Princess thought about that. She regarded Jesse with curiosity. "Maybe they are," she replied.

"I have 'knowing' of the Land of Air," I reminded her, "and so does my brother!"

"Then you must find the truth of your way," the Princess explained, with that superior tone my mother used when I was being difficult.

"Oh, really?" I replied sarcastically. "Gosh! And do you mind telling me what exactly is the 'truth' of my way?"

Jesse smirked. "Maggie doesn't like the truth."

Look who was talking!

The Princess turned to me with her you'll-understand-this-someday smile. "The truth is said to lie in the source of light," she repeated for the zillionth time.

"Uh-huh," I nodded. "Can you move like Pyrope can?"

The Princess hesitated, and I knew instantly that she could.

"You can, can't you?" I demanded.

She shook her head. "I cannot move to your world," she replied. "I don't know your world, so I can't visualize it."

"But if I told you?" I insisted. "If I described it?"

"Only you can move, from *inside* yourself," she explained.

Nodding his head in agreement, the Basalt Guard coughed up another hairball. "It is against Rock Rule 639-B!" he blurted.

I was really annoyed with this doofus and his too many muscles.

Gneiss was too. "You got a name?" he snapped.

The Guard considered the question.

"You can call me BAZ,'" he replied, sounding like pouring gravel.

Playing with the sound of his name, Torri sighed, "Baazz. Is that short foah 'Bahsalt,' Mistuh Baazz?" she purred, batting her eyelashes at him. "Do you mahnd if ah lean on you, Baazz? Ah sudd'nly feel sooo weak!"

I wanted to know what made this Baz such an expert. "What exactly are you doing here, Baz?" I demanded.

"I was CHO-sen," he proudly replied and stood a bit taller.

Gneiss guffawed in disbelief. "You were chosen? For what—ta get crushed?"

Out of the corner of my eye, I spied a small shadow that seemed to skitter after Scheelite's light.

"Could you move us to the Land of Magma?" Jesse asked the Princess.

"No!" I cried. "I'm not going to any Land of Magma!" Pointing at Gneiss, I argued, "He said they don't even know if this God-Wizard is real. He said that they're told to believe. They don't know anything for certain!"

"Well, I believe," Jesse insisted stubbornly.

"In what?" I cried. "That the pile of rocks in your room can save our mother?"

"They can!" insisted Jesse.

"No, they can't!" I yelled at him. "Nobody can! She's dying, okay?"

There. I'd finally said those awful words. They hung like daggers in the air, and suddenly I hated myself and Jesse and the whole world.

Jesse looked as if I'd slapped him. "You just want her to die so you can be right!" he protested, choking back tears.

I couldn't stop myself. My anger rose even more, and it felt good to be able to lash out at him.

"I am right, jerk, and deep down you know it!"

Another shadow slithered after Scheelite's light.

"Oh, God!" I blurted, pointing at it. "It moved!"

"What moved?" yipped Gneiss.

Jesse peered into the shadows. "It's a fossil, stupid," he sniffled as he inspected it closer. "A fossil of a centipede!" he squeaked in amazement.

"A centipede?" Pyrope inquired fearfully.

"It moved!" I hissed. "Why did it move?"

"It mooov'd?" Torri crooned as Scheelite grabbed hold of her, eyes wide with fear.

Examining the other shadows, Jesse exclaimed, "They're *all* fossils!"

"That's why it's called FOSS-illiaa," Baz rasped.

Leaning in for a better look, Jesse gasped, "There! What's that?" He pointed at a dent in the rock, and his voice spiked. "It looks like . . . the fossil of an *eye*! There's a beak and . . . a part of a claw?" he whispered, as if he didn't want to wake them.

Now everybody had to lean in for a closer look.

"I bet it's a pterosaur!" Jesse exclaimed excitedly.

"'Terrosaw'?" mimicked Pyrope hesitantly.

"A flying reptile, like a prehistoric bird," replied Jesse.

"Oh!" Torri inhaled apprehensively. "A buuhd?"

"An animal with wings!" I answered impatiently.

She looked at me as if I were speaking Chinese. Why was I even trying to explain this to her? "Wings! You know—so it can fly? In the air?"

"Flah?" she asked, totally befuddled. Maybe she really was as dense as her drawl.

"To move in the air," Jesse patiently explained.

Nodding his head grimly, Gneiss grumbled, "Crushed boids, dat's what we'll be."

Torri held on to herself and leaned in for a closer look. Her light fell directly on the fossil of the eye and it blinked.

It *blinked*!

An orange eyeball with a black slit down the middle snapped open and was staring back at us!

"Oh mahhh!" Torri gasped.

A sudden burst of light flashed overhead.

"What wazzat?" Gneiss yelped. "Did y'see dat?"

A high whining sound split the dark, and there was another flash as a fiery light streaked overhead and disappeared into the shadow forest.

There was a small gust of wind, then another streak of light, and another.

One was coming straight at us!

Protecting the Princess, Baz frantically waved his arms about and the light veered away at the last second.

A larger one shot off in another direction, followed by a bigger gust of wind and an awful screeching sound.

More lights streaked past, and the silhouettes of the shadow trees started to move in the swirling wind.

Scheelite ran to Pyrope as Baz held on to Princess Amethyst and leaned into the gusts that were nearly knocking them over.

Flashing with bursts of color, more fossil shadows of half-formed snakes, flattened rats, and squished birds slithered and scurried about as the streaking lights passed over them. The longer the light lasted, the more the fossil shadows came to life. Their bodies filled out and blossomed with an array of colors as they skittered farther and flew higher in pursuit of the light, until they were sucked back into their dark silhouettes with piercing shrieks.

"They're after our light!" yelled Jesse. "The light gives them life!"

Grabbing Pyrope's arm, Scheelite pointed behind them. "Look!" she squealed.

A huge fossil shadow was actually flying! It looked like a half-eaten giant Dragonfly flickering with iridescent colors as it erratically chased after the streaking lights. As it caught one, the Dragonfly's undersides erupted in an explosion of colors that coursed through its entire body.

A blast of wind turned me around, and I saw that the fossil shadow of the huge Pterosaur was peeling its enormous wings from the rock.

The creature's torn skin flickered brightly, and its flattened body swelled as, with a great shriek, it flew straight up and snatched the Dragonfly in its jagged beak. Swallowing it whole, the Pterosaur blossomed into brilliant yellows and greens and grew even larger, then veered away with a deafening screech and banked sharply toward Torri's flashing colors.

Torri stood frozen, mesmerized by the flying creature.

"De're gonna eat us!" Gneiss screamed.

"RUUNN!" yelled Baz.

Pyrope grabbed Scheelite by the hand.

I turned to run but the ground jumped up at me with a massive jolt and I lost my balance.

"Torri!" I yelled as another jolt brought me to my knees.

Torri couldn't move.

Gneiss did an about-face and struggled against the violently jumping ground to get back to her.

Ignoring two of the golden lights that streaked past its head, the Pterosaur leaned on its massive wings, swooped sideways, and dove at Torri with a terrifying screech.

Suddenly there was a deafening roar.

Crashing out of a grove of shadow trees, the fossil shadow of a Giganotosaurus was charging right at Pyrope and Scheelite!

In four thundering strides, the Giganotosaurus snatched the Pterosaur out of the air with its great jaws. Shaking the flying reptile like a rag doll, the huge dinosaur was instantly infused with a brilliant cascade of colors.

"GO BACK!" Baz screamed at Pyrope as he ran to help Torri.

Distracted by their vibrating light, the Giganotosaurus released the barely flickering reptile and roared at Pyrope and Scheelite. Then he charged as Pyrope half dragged, half pulled Scheelite past Torri, who was still unable to move.

"Run!" Pyrope screamed at Torri.

Jesse ran to help.

"JESSE!" I screamed in horror. He was going to get killed!

Opening its massive mouth, the horrible creature drove its horrid head at Torri.

A beam of light hit its eye.

Lurching sideways, the huge creature snapped at the light, which split again and again into a chaotic crash of ricocheting rays.

Jesse was trying to distract the beast with the flashlight!

The newly created light storm immediately grew and caused the wind to blow even harder.

The Giganotosaurus raged, twisting about and angrily lashing out at the splintering beams that were shooting past its head.

Baz reached Torri, lifted her onto his shoulder, and started back toward us.

"Jesse!" I shouted. "The light! Turn off the light!"

Turning off the flashlight, Jesse hollered to Baz, "RUN! RUN!"

Gneiss ran to help Baz as the dinosaur wheeled about, bellowed, and charged them.

Jesse grabbed my hand, and Baz handed off Torri to Gneiss.

The Princess's foot caught an outcropping of rock.

Slowly spinning, she reached out for Baz, but he had turned to face the charging beast and she fell to the ground.

"Princess Amethyst!" Jesse screamed, running back for her.

The Giganotosaurus opened its huge jaws and lunged.

Baz didn't budge.

We watched in horror as Jesse covered the Princess with his body, and the flashing jaws engulfed Baz . . . then turned into shadows and *passed right through him*!

With piercing screeches and cries, the dinosaur and other fossil shadows were being sucked back into the shadow forest, their screams swallowed by the howling wind.

Then it stopped.

Gneiss fell to his knees, spent as Torri's colors flashed out of control.

The streaking golden lights had vanished, and the shadow world became eerily quiet.

Guarding the edge of our circle of light, Baz watched the last glimmers of the fossil shadows squeak and slide into the darkness.

Vibrating with light, Pyrope carried Scheelite over to us. "What now?" he asked hoarsely.

Scheelite was shaking violently. I reached to help her and realized that I was shaking as well.

As if being swallowed by a Giganotosaurus were a daily occurrence, Baz gargled calmly, "The correct action would be to-GO."

"Ta where, Mr. Information?" choked Gneiss.

"Look!" exclaimed Jesse.

Two of the streaking lights that had started this whole thing were floating high above us. More circled above them as the larger of the two darted back toward us, then away.

"Don't move!" whispered the Princess.

His mica rippling every which way, Gneiss gasped, "Oh, sure! Let's just stay here and wait for da next fossil creature to come for lunch!"

The larger light came closer. It was a pulsing golden glob with something dark at its center.

"It's amber!" cried Jesse.

"'Ambuh'? What's ambuh'?" Torri squeaked.

"Petrified tree sap," Jesse replied in a hushed voice.

The Amber came still closer. The thing inside was the size of a small dog and looked like some kind of large insect with a very long needle sticking out of its face.

"It's a m-mosquito!" stammered Jesse excitedly. "A *prehistoric mosquito!*"

Still trying to catch his breath, Gneiss gulped, "A what?"

"Uh mahskeetuh? Oh, mah!" Torri exclaimed, not having a clue.

"What does it want?" Scheelite cried.

Rotating forward, the Amber Mosquito floated toward me. Even though it was stuck in the amber with its horrible stinger-thing, I felt as if it were looking right at me. It was getting brighter and brighter the closer it came to me. I wanted to wave it away, but I was afraid to move.

Then came the horrible screeches of the fossil shadows, reawakened by the growing light.

"They're comin' back!" Gneiss cried.

"What's happening?" I demanded as the monstrous mosquito kept coming at me. "Somebody tell me what's happening!"

"The closer it gets to you, the brighter it glows!" Jesse exclaimed.

I could feel my face, my neck—my whole body—getting really warm. I couldn't breathe, it was so close.

"What's it doing?" I hissed, jerking my head to the side. I was starting to burn up.

It throbbed even brighter.

"Don't move!" bossed Jesse.

It was nearly touching me. "Get it away from me!" I shrieked.

In a flash it streaked back up to the other Ambers and joined a six-sided cluster that instantly surged with the prehistoric Mosquito's new light.

"Why did you do that?" Jesse yelled at me, as if I was supposed to let it smother me.

"You try standing there and getting burned!" I challenged.

The screams of the fossil shadows were growing louder.

"We got a more pressin' problem!" Gneiss yelped.

The Amber Mosquito darted toward us again, then away. It kept moving back and forth between us and the other Ambers.

"What's it doing?" Jesse wondered aloud, as if we had time for a discussion.

"Maybe it wants us to follow them," replied the Princess.

And that's precisely what Jesse did.

"Where are you going?" I cried in confusion.

"They have light!" Jesse answered simply and kept walking.

"So do we! Let the fossil things follow them!"

"Where'd they get it, smarty-pants?" he shouted back, as though he knew everything.

"From when we turned on the flashlight, dummy!"

He began running after the Ambers. "The flashlight didn't make the mosquito glow brighter when it came close to you!" he replied. "There's something more, something besides the flashlight!"

Shouting after Jesse through the growing shrieks and

screeches, Gneiss appealed in a panic, "Ya really tink we should do dat? They seem to be attractin' some very large—"

"So are we," reminded Pyrope, as he pulled Scheelite to her feet, grabbed Torri, and started after Jesse.

Helping the Princess up, Baz warned, "King's Rock Rule 243-C: It may be a trAAP!"

"What kahnda trap?" Torri asked breathlessly, her colors flashing in alarm as she held on to Pyrope.

The Princess started after Jesse as well. "Jesse's right," she claimed. "There is something more—something besides the batteries that made you and your brother glow."

"I wasn't glowing!" I insisted, as Baz dutifully followed the Princess, leaving only Gneiss and me.

The screams were getting closer.

"What are we gonna do?" Gneiss cried out in dismay.

I could still hear Baz continuing his analysis.

"It could be a FLAN-king move. King's Rock Rule 119-E: 'A primary de-CEPTIONN where one side fakes a re-TREET . . .'"

I wanted to let them go. I wanted to be rid of Jesse and this whole nightmare, but I couldn't wake up.

He had the flashlight. I had to follow him.

THE GIFT OF LIGHT

"We were driving Mom home from the hospital
for the last time, and Jesse kept asking when we
could stop for ice cream.

"It's over the next hill," Daddy kept saying, then
acted all surprised when it wasn't there.

Eventually Jesse gave up and collapsed back into
the warmth of Mom's blanket, and they both fell
asleep in the backseat.

I watched the occasional headlights flash across
my father's haunted eyes as he stared helplessly into
the night.

Our crystal light was fading.

Darting in and out of thinning tree shadows, the Ambers
were getting farther and farther away.

There were fewer fossil shadows following us. Screeching
their hunger, they disappeared into the blackness behind us,
leaving small tornadoes of flashing dust and whispering flurries
in the growing quiet.

"Jesse! Stop!" I called, determined to keep up with him.

"We can't," he yelled back. "We can't lose the Ambers' light!"

"We don't need their light, Jesse. We have the flashlight!"

Struggling to keep up with me, Gneiss mica splotches looked dirty and dull. "How far we goin'?" He groaned weakly, "It's gettin' darker."

He waddled beside me in silence. "Ya know," he continued, clearing his throat, "you tink da way I tink, and I tink da way you tink," he declared. "Maybe we're, y'know, related?" he ventured, meeting my look of disbelief with a dusty shrug.

"Yeah, right," I snorted.

"No," he insisted, "maybe da Princess has a point; we *do* kinda look alike."

I walked faster, closing the distance between Jesse and us. Unfortunately, Gneiss managed to keep up.

"You say tings dat I'm tinkin'. I tink tings dat you're sayin'," he rattled on. "Why is dat? And look at Torri; she don't look so much like ya, but she definitely has moves."

Stopping him right there, I demanded in disgust, "Are you saying I have 'moves'?" I couldn't believe I was having this conversation with a squashed rock. What made him think I was like that?

"You're a goil," he shrugged. "Goils have moves," he concluded brilliantly. "Ya don' tink ya have moves?"

I wasn't about to acknowledge his question with a reply.

"The next thing you'll tell me is that I'm related to the Princess!" I blurted and stomped away.

Catching up with me, he limped alongside and actually kept his mouth shut.

Silence never felt so good.

"I tink dere are parts of her dat ya'd like to be like," he stated confidently.

"Oh, really?" I snapped sarcastically. "She reminds me of my mother!"

Waving one of his rock hands, he counseled, "Well, if da rock fits . . ."

As if he were even close! I wasn't "just like Scheelite," or anything like Torri. Okay, Pyrope and Jesse were both definitely dumb and stubborn, and even though Baz had his rules the same as Jesse did, what about King Bloo? Did that mean I was like the Emerald Queen of Green? Why had she said that thing about my teeth and about us being more alike than I could believe? And the Red Prince, who was he like? And the Orange Prince, and Pyrite—and, and, and . . . ? Why was I even thinking about this? None of it was real, but I couldn't get away. It was like when the monster is about to get you in a nightmare and you can't get your legs to move.

Gneiss tripped and brushed against me, getting his dull mica all over my arm.

"Suppose dere was anodder way," he suggested, brushing his mica dandruff off of me with his clumpy hands. "If you could get your hands on, ya know, da flishlight—"

"Flashlight," I corrected him.

"Dat's what I said, da flishlight. Now, just supposin' we, uh, went back to da Kingdom of Beryl wid da flishlight—"

"Flashlight, and duh—they'd kill us!"

"Not if we had da light," he replied with a knowing look.

Had I heard him correctly? I waited for him to continue.

"Light's been fadin' back dere for a while," he confided. "Nobody talks about it, but everyone's scared of it. Now, if we had da flishlight, if we came back *wid* da light . . ." he paused, then shrugged, "den maybe da Holy Clear wouldn't have any choice but to be more, y'know, helpful."

"But he doesn't know the Land of Air," I reminded His Denseness.

"Ahh!" he exclaimed, as if he had a big secret. "Nobody really knows what His Clearness knows or doesn't know," he insinuated, raising a mica-crusted eyebrow, "if ya know what I mean."

"And he could send us home?" I asked, keeping my voice down and hoping against hope.

He wagged his head back and forth.

"It's a real possibility," he allowed. "I like it better dan runnin' around da Land of Magma lookin' for dis Wizard of Iz, who, let me remind you, nobody's ever seen!"

He lowered his voice even more as if he were afraid of being overheard by Jesse and the Princess. "An' ya could take whomever ya wanted, ya know, wid ya, to Land of Air." He shrugged. "Just tinkin'."

"And you could move us to Beryl?" I asked. "Do you know how?"

Averting his eyes, he mumbled, "I, ah, I'm workin' on dat."

Fine, I thought. That's just great. "I thought everybody knew how to move."

Taking another glance around, he leaned in and whispered, "Well, actually, most have forgotten, movin' bein' outlawed and all. Dat and it takes a lotta light—a lotta light. But no problem," he quickly added, "some people still know how to move. You and I are not da only ones dat wanna get outta here."

"The flashlight—" I thought out loud. It would serve Jesse right.

"If ya could get ya hands on it," he repeated, nodding emphatically.

Steal the flashlight from Jesse?

I watched him and the Princess walking just ahead of us.

What would happen to him? Could I do that to him? I found myself thinking about what it would be like if I were rid of him. Well, he *was* being pigheaded about trying to find this Metamorphia place, and I sure wasn't going to go on some fool's errand. Then I thought about Mom and Dad, and I guessed I could come back and save him if it came to that.

Gneiss suddenly had a prance to his step. "Y'know, sometimes you gotta tink outside da crystal, ya know?" he shrugged. "Me? I'm creative. Ya got a problem? I'm your guy." He smiled and patted himself on the chest, creating a small explosion of mica dust.

The Ambers floated even farther off, and the light from our crystal people was getting weaker. There were hardly any more shadow trees in the growing darkness. There was no wind and only the occasional screech of a distant fossil shadow. Fewer spots of mica light sparkled on the looming shadowy shapes of rock formations.

I watched Jesse doggedly walking ahead with Princess Amethyst beside him and Baz following at a respectable distance.

I could only see the back of Jesse's head as he trudged along, but I knew his jaw was stubbornly set in determination, his eyes fixed on the shrinking Ambers.

Then I heard the Princess talking to him as if I were right next to her.

Confused, I stopped and looked around. I couldn't understand how their voices sounded so close as they got farther and farther away.

How? How was I doing this?

A wave of fear rolled through me.

"Why did the Amber Mosquito grow brighter when it came close to Maggie?" the Princess inquired.

"I don't know," Jesse answered. "Maybe it's the batteries. If their light is failing—"

"Maggie has no batteries," interrupted the Princess. "There's something else," she suggested, studying Jesse, "perhaps something inside you as humans."

"You sound like my mother," Jesse observed sadly. "There's nothing inside me."

"Not even your faith?"

"I don't understand faith," Jesse snipped. "If I did, I wouldn't be here."

Smiling, the Princess asked, "Does your mother have a lot of light?"

I knew that Jesse was tired of questions. He wanted answers; how were they ever going to get home, how long had they been down here, would our mother still be alive if and when we got back?

Jesse stopped to watch us as we struggled to catch up.

"My mother's dying," he replied in a small voice.

"What is 'dying'?" the Princess asked.

I knew Jesse didn't want to talk about this. Why did he have to talk about this? Was it going to change anything?

"When life stops," he finally replied, "when it comes to an end."

The Princess thought about that. "How does it come to an end?" she asked.

Jesse watched the fading Ambers getting smaller and dimmer. I knew that he was afraid that he wasn't going to find the source of light. It sure wasn't his flashlight; that he knew. That's all he knew.

"Everything comes to an end," he answered bitterly and continued after the Ambers.

"You mean everything changes," the Princess suggested softly.

Jesse stopped and challenged her. "Into what?" he asked impatiently.

The Princess shrugged. "Into what it was before—into what it's going to become?"

"Well, I don't want my mother to change," Jesse growled as he continued after the Ambers. "I just want everything to stay as it is!"

Watching him march away, the Princess smiled sadly. "Yes," she said quietly, following Jesse with Baz at her shoulder. "That is something a part of all of us wants."

Scheelite's yellow splashes of light had turned to sluggish mustard. She leaned on Pyrope, whose crystals had become chalky and gray.

Torri's color was nearly gone. She had talked Baz into carrying her piggyback, and he trudged along with her on board, muttering to himself.

"Jesse!" I yelled. "We can hardly see! Turn on the flash— OW!" I yelped in pain as I banged my toe on something hard.

Scheelite pointed into the darkness ahead. "The Ambers, the Ambers!" she rasped.

The disappearing lights of the Ambers were scarcely illuminating the edge of a cliff high above us.

Faint silhouettes of ragged grooves and deep gouges climbed the great wall like ancient tree bark. Sparse, branchlike arms, broken and twisted, reached out from the face of the cliff into the surrounding darkness where our fading light was barely reflected by scattered patches of mica.

"Are they gone?" Scheelite inquired fearfully.

His own light pulsing weakly, Pyrope helped her sit on the dark ground.

The Princess leaned on Baz, and we watched helplessly as the Ambers vanished, leaving only a trace of light.

"We've got to turn on the flashlight, Jesse!" I cried. "The Ambers'll come to the light. We can't follow them if we can't see them."

Hardly visible in the dim light, Jesse was running his hands along the jagged cliff face. "Not yet," he insisted.

Shivering in panic, Scheelite held on to Pyrope's arm. "If we turn it on, won't the fossil shadows come to the flashlight?" she asked, her voice squeaking.

"There's gotta be a way around!" Jesse persisted, feeling his way in the failing light. "There's gotta be!"

"Why?" I demanded angrily. "Just 'cause you say so?"

Gneiss groaned. "First da darkness, den da crushin'," he predicted gravely, his head nodding with only an occasional glint of mica.

"Fossils aren't made by crushing," Jesse replied.

Even in the growing darkness, I could hear his voice quiver with fear.

"Fossils are made over hundreds of thousands of years," he recited, sounding like one of his books. "Rocks and minerals are deposited in layers and things get preserved inside like a sandwich when the—"

"Uh 'sanwich'?" interrupted Torri. "What kahnd of thangs?" she nervously asked.

"Animals, plants, everything that used to be alive," Jesse answered, hanging on to all his useless information.

Grabbing Scheelite and Torri, who still had some dim light exuding from them, I dragged them over to Jesse. We looked like ghosts floating in darkness.

"You don't know everything, Jesse Cooper!" I snapped and reached into his pocket for the flashlight.

Pushing me away, he argued, "I do know that the Land of Air isn't hell. It's a heaven! Our heaven! It's a land full of beautiful things and light and people and animals and . . . and . . ." His eyes were blinking quickly like when he was about to cry.

"So what?" I replied angrily. "We're stuck down here! Who cares what you know?"

I grabbed for the flashlight again.

Wrenching it away, he yelped, "There's another way! Something more!" he stubbornly insisted.

"There is nothing more, Jesse!" I screamed at him. "There is no Wizard of Iz, no magic fairy who's gonna make everything okay! OKAY? If you don't turn on the light, it will be dark forever, and we'll never see our mother again! Is that what you want?"

"Batteries are not the source of light!" Jesse cried. "The flashlight is only temporary. We need to preserve it till we find the true source." Tears ran down his face as he stuffed the flashlight deep into his pocket and turned back to the wall.

In the gathering darkness I could hear him fighting to swallow his sobs. Barely able to see his shaking shoulders, I wondered for a moment if that's what I looked like when I was crying. I realized how young my baby brother was and I felt sad for him. I reached out to touch his shoulder.

"Maybe it's time to turn it on." I gently suggested, trying my best to talk to him as our mother would when he was upset.

"NO!" he cried, throwing off my hand and moving farther along the cliff face, nearly disappearing in the darkness. "We have to wait."

"For what?" I exploded. "What are we waiting for?"

My question hung in the stillness.

"I don't know—okay?" his voice came back, high and thin.

Fear filled my belly, and I wanted to grab him and shake him till his teeth rattled.

"Dey tink he's a god," Gneiss whispered in my ear.

"Geez!" I gasped in suprise.

"'Cuz he has da flishlight," he wheezed, his voice sounding like scratching rocks.

"Flashlight. It's a flashlight!"

"Dat's right, flishlight. It makes da light. Just like you said." He pulled me aside. "Listen, our world has never been widdout light. If dey believe dat your Land of Air is indeed a heaven of light, dey could believe you got special powers. Ya know, dat you are gods!" He paused . . . and then asked pointedly, "Are you gods, cousin?"

The way he said it scared me.

"Jesse," the Princess gently called, "what do you believe you should do? What are your choices?"

"Choices . . . I've got choices," Jesse muttered to himself "I've got choices . . ."

"It's getting DARKer," Baz quietly rasped.

"Jesse?" the Princess asked.

"I don't know," Jesse whined. "A part of me feels as if I should wait, then another part of me—"

"We can't make a decision on a feeling!" I shouted.

"We're lost!" Scheelite blurted.

"No! We can't be lost!" Jesse insisted vehemently. "There's got to be—"

Z-Z-I-I-N-N-G!

A needle of light split the dark between us.

Zing! . . . Zing! There was another . . . and another!

My heart leapt.

High above us, a blindingly bright object was slowly emerging from the surface of the gouged cliff. More needles of light zinged down on us as it grew larger and larger, till there were hundreds, thousands, of thin rays showering us in one great shaft of light.

"Holy mica!" cried Gneiss.

A violent blast of wind brought the awakening cry of the fossil shadows.

"Fossils!" Scheelite cried.

The light above seemed to be descending. It was coming down on us!

Princess Amethyst turned brilliantly violet.

Torri began popping all her colors, and Pyrope and Scheelite became incandescent.

Baz and Gneiss sparkled and vibrated so much that they couldn't move.

Trying to peer into the light, all I could see was a huge ball of amber, so bright it was nearly white. There was something inside it, something larger than an insect—much larger.

Two sprawling sticks became running legs caught in midstride. Two arms reached out in desperation, and long black hair wrapped about a face, its mouth frozen in a scream, its eyes wide with fear.

It looked like one of those prehistoric people I'd seen in the displays at the natural history museum. It was! It was a prehistoric girl wrapped in a ratty animal hide, and somehow caught, preserved in amber, while running in terror from something.

The amber orb rotated forward, and the Amber Girl's eyes moved in my direction even though they were dead, staring out at nothing.

"Wh-what d-does it w-want?" Gneiss stuttered.

A piercing chorus of screeches erupted from the awakening fossil shadows in the surrounding darkness. I could see their twisted shapes frantically flickering and scrambling over each other to get to the Amber Girl's light.

"They're coming!" Scheelite cried. "They're coming!"

Smaller Ambers began to appear from behind the Amber Girl. Hundreds, thousands of them! Whirring and whining like crying insects, they began to swarm and move into us, getting louder and louder.

My body started to vibrate!

Trying to spin away from them, Torri held her arms above her head. "Whut aah they dooin'?" she wailed.

Gneiss tried to wave them away. "Hey! Stop pushin'!" he yelled in panic.

I couldn't . . . I couldn't feel my body. *Oh God*, I thought, *am I dying?* I opened my mouth to scream, and my voice came out like slow syrup.

"They're crushing us!" Scheelite screamed.

Raising a dazzling hand, Baz commanded, "Hold your GROU-nnd!"

"You hold it!" Gneiss howled, his voice sounding like it was coming from the far end of a long tunnel, and tried to turn away from the thousands of nudging and shoving Ambers.

We were floating! Floating through . . . through . . . ?

I looked in panic for Jesse.

Something was very different about him in the brilliant white of the light.

His face . . . his clothes . . . they were . . . *I could see right through him!* I could see the insides of the wall right through his body. He was transparent.

I looked down at my own hands—they were moving through the inside of the cliff! I could barely see their shape but I couldn't feel them . . . and I could see right through them!

We had become the cliff, and the cliff had become us.

The weird sound of the Ambers was changing. It was becoming . . . like thousands of high voices singing in harmony . . . vibrating in every part of me!

Drifting past with the Princess and Gneiss, Jesse was like a statue . . . slowly turning with a look of surprise on his face . . . the crystals he'd collected floating out of his pockets along with the flashlight.

Torri gently twirled past, and Scheelite floated right through Pyrope as the outlines of their bodies blended with each other and the insides of the cliff.

I felt weightless and warm—peaceful, as if there weren't a bit of difference between me, and everything that wasn't me.

Then the singing voices were becoming a high whine again.

Small flecks and whisker-thin shadows appeared in a translucent surface. Flickering and drifting like specks of dust when you close your eyes to the sun, their black silhouettes vibrated against the whiteness and suddenly blossomed into all kinds of colors, washing and whipping through the blinding brightness. Ribbons of colored light waved across and through each other, undulating like a brilliantly billowing gown.

The nearly white light of the Ambers was darkening to gold, and my body was feeling heavier. A deep sadness welled up inside me as if I had found, and then lost, the most precious thing in life.

I reached in front of me and realized that my hands weren't transparent any longer.

The rolling translucent surface had become a swelling

pearlescent wall, rippling with rainbows. Fingers of golden light spilled out from a twisted thatch of radiant opal roots at its base and ran in rivulets into darkened depths.

"The cliff is a wall!" Jesse gasped. "It's a wall of petrified trees!"

"Da t-t-trees are p-petrified?" cried Gneiss, his teeth chattering.

Glistening brilliantly, Pyrope carefully reached out and touched the pearly surface. Small waves of light rolled up his arm.

Torri gushed with color and shook uncontrollably as Baz inspected the wall and Scheelite leaned with a sigh into the light that was pouring through her.

"We went through the wall!" Jesse whispered, running his fingers over the smooth surface. "We . . . we moved!"

"We . . . what happened?" I croaked. I felt as if all my molecules were vibrating and crashing into each other. I felt giddy and short of breath, and I didn't know whether to laugh in relief or cry from a sense of loss that came from some dark place inside me.

"Don't you see? The cliff is made of trees!" Jesse gushed, gulping at his breath. "Trees that once lived in the air—you know, above. Ancient trees that once were alive!" he sputtered. "They must've been buried all at once—by a volcano or an earthquake or something—and they became petrified wood. They became opal. Fire opal!"

A great burst of buzzes, clicks, and whines erupted behind us.

The Amber Girl was floating in the middle of a constellation of smaller Ambers, which had spread out behind her like the stars of the Milky Way. The closer ones vibrated with white light and had insects inside them. Darker ones, which had nothing at all inside, faded even as we watched, gently bouncing off the brighter ones till they fell lightless to the ground.

"Look, inside! It's a bee!" Jesse exclaimed and pointed at another, "And a butterfly!"

"A 'bee'?" asked Pyrope in confusion.

Baz was instantly on alert. "'BUUD-derfly'?" he burped.

Gneiss stared in horror at a prehistoric ant as large as a cat, which was floating up to him.

"Get lost!" Gneiss yelped.

The bee came up to Baz. "Get aWAAYY! SHOOO!" he commanded, trying to wave it away.

Then, a high sing-songy voice seemed to surround us.

Away-away . . .

Get-away-now . . .

Shoo-a-bee, shoo-a-bee,

Shoo-a-me-how?

Was it the Amber Girl? Her mouth wasn't moving, and her eyes were locked in a frozen stare, even though they seemed to be looking right at me.

"She's singing!" whispered Jesse.

"How?" I smirked. "She's not moving her mouth!"

How-in-me-come-from-me

Light-in-me-now?

Light-in-me-moves-in-me,

Moves-in-me-how?

"Is thaht lahk uh foruhn language?" asked Torri, unimpressed by a singing dead girl. "Cause ah cayn't unduhstan' a word uh whut she's singin'."

"It's all rock ta me," Gneiss muttered, shaking his head.

"Are you alive?" Jesse asked the Amber Girl.

Her amber orb rotated toward him and she sang:

Light-in-me,

Light-in-me,

Light-in-me-how?

Light-is-alive

In-amber-me-how?

"Maybe she's trying to tell us, or ask us, something," Jesse wondered.

"She's . . . not . . . moving . . . her . . . mouth!" I enunciated slowly in Jesse's face.

"Well, tell her ta spit it out," Gneiss grumped, "I'm getting a rockache listenin' ta her."

The Amber Girl rotated toward him.

Spit-it-out,

Spit-it-out,

Spit-it-out-now.

Spit-it-out-rock-ache,

Spit-it-out-how?

Nervously waving her off, Gneiss shrugged his mica shoulders. "Sorry, Lady of da Sap. Forget it. Slip-a da m-mineral," he mumbled.

Sap-is-me,

Sap-is-me . . .

She floated closer to him.

Round-me-somehow.

Sap-is-me,

Alive-in-me,

Tree-sap-somehow . . .

"She keeps saying 'how,'" Jesse wondered out loud. "Maybe she wants to know how we have light!" he exclaimed excitedly.

Chirping and clicking even louder, the smaller Ambers

floated closer to Pyrope, who playfully waved his hand through them as they dodged and danced around him like fireflies.

"Hey, look at this!" he laughed.

"They're so cute!" Scheelite squealed. "They're playing!"

Gneiss ducked as two small Ambers darted at him. "Oy! Dis we don' need," he groaned unhappily.

I turned to find the Amber Girl floating closer to me and pulsing brighter. I started feeling warmer, a lot warmer.

Her voice softly sang:

Light-a-me,

Light-a-me,

In-a-me-now . . .

Light-a-me-in-a-me,

In-a-me-how?

"Look into my eyes!" I pleaded. "The light is not *in* me!"

"She is looking into your eyes," Princess Amethyst replied. "Maybe she sees something."

"You both have DNA!" Jesse blurted.

"DNA?" I echoed dumbly, scared by how hot I was becoming. The Amber Girl's light was so brilliant that her body had turned white. I felt as if I were burning up. I couldn't breathe.

Jesse turned excitedly to the others. "No, really!" he continued. "Scientists can actually make life from the DNA of dead insects preserved in amber. She's got DNA, and Maggie's got DNA. Maybe her DNA *sees* your DNA?"

"Is dat appropriate?" asked Gneiss.

I turned my face from the Amber Girl, but her light was all around me.

"Maybe that's why the Ambers with the insects inside them get brighter when they come near you," suggested Princess Amethyst.

"This is ridiculous," I replied, panicking. "She doesn't see me, my DNA, or anything! She's dead. She doesn't see. She, she—"

"She's looking at you right now," the Princess observed, "and you're glowing."

"No, I am not!"

"Wow!" exclaimed Jesse.

"Ohhh, look at yuh!" Torri gushed, pointing a Popsicle finger at me, "Yuh all rehd! Yuh look sooo pretty!"

I felt overwhelmed, as if the Amber Girl were filling me with her light and finding out everything about me . . .

My fear reared up, and I lashed out in panic. "Stop staring at me!" I shouted.

Immediately her amber orb jumped back, causing a rippling wave through the surrounding Ambers, and something pulled at me, something sad, and it frightened me.

"Don't do that!" Jesse cried. "You're scaring her."

I couldn't talk.

Jesse looked closer at me, and his face changed.

"Are you all right?" Jesse asked, awkwardly. "You look like you're about to cry,"

"I'm fine, and no, I'm not going to cry!" I lied.

Grunting, Gneiss asked, "So, what's dis DNA, and where can a rock get it?"

"Can aah have sum of yuh dee-inn-ay?" Torri cooed, batting her eyelashes at me.

"You can't just get DNA," Jesse explained. "Maggie is not a rock. She's a human. The prehistoric girl preserved in tree sap is, or was, human and has always had DNA. See, DNA is information," he continued, "like a map of life for plants and animals. Rocks don't have it."

"Isn't dat discrimination?" grumbled Gneiss.

Slowly nodding her head, the Princess tried to understand. "So, her 'information' is knowing Maggie's 'information'?"

"NO! No, no, no, NO!" I shouted. I couldn't stand this anymore. I turned on the Amber Girl. "Get away! Get away from me!"

Backing farther away, she rotated forward as if she were bowing to me.

"No! Wait . . ." Jesse called to her.

"And I am *not* pretty!" I barked at Torri. "And I don't feel anything, okay?" I yelled at Scheelite, and pointing at the Amber Girl, I cried, "And she—it—is dead. Got it? *Dead!*"

But she wouldn't stop her singing!

Maggie-me, Maggie-me,

Hear-a-me-now—

"NO!" I screamed and covered my ears.

"Please—don't go!" Jesse pleaded with her.

Turn-your-back,

Turn-your-back-and-see-how . . .

I couldn't stop her voice! It was as if it were coming from inside me.

I could see the Princess talking to me—I could see her lips moving—but all I could hear was the voice of the Amber Girl as she backed away.

Turn-from-your-heart

And-you-will-cry-now.

"I don't care what she's saying!" I yelled at her, my hands still clamped to my ears.

Pulling my arms down, Jesse shouted, "You're scaring her away! There's something here!" He called to the Amber Girl, "Come back . . . please! Please come back!"

She disappeared into her cloud of Ambers.

Jesse wheeled on me with his foul breath. "See?" he cried.

"There's nothing here!" I screamed at him. "No Wizard of Iz. Nothing! Nothing except rocks and more rocks, and I want to go home!"

"You felt it!" Jesse insisted vehemently. "You know you felt it! I felt it. There's something with the light, something besides the light!"

"I didn't feel anything!" I lied and held out my hand. "Give me the flashlight, Jesse!"

"No!" he cried. "There is something besides the light. Something that creates the light!"

"Good," I answered curtly. "You go and find it, and give me the flashlight."

Sticking out his chin, he whined, "You can't just close your eyes and pretend there isn't something, Maggie! You can't just give up!"

"There is nothing else!" I shouted in his dumb face. "You're not going to find anything, and our mom's going to die and we're never going to see her again. We're going to be stuck down here forever!"

"Don't say that!" he threatened. "You don't know that!"

"Yes, I do!" I was so angry I was crying. "And if you don't, you're even stupider than I thought!"

"I hate you, Maggie!" he cried through his tears.

"And I hate you!" I spat back. "I've hated you since you were born. You're a selfish brat, and you don't care about anybody but yourself!"

And I ran. I didn't care where, or if I ever saw my brother again. I ran in the only direction I could—after the disappearing light of the Ambers.

LETTING GO

I was always holding on.

I held on to old clothes, old toys . . . grudges.

Even when Daddy let Jesse and me take turns driving Molly and Blue, I held on to their reins too tightly, and Jesse would call me a "spaz."

I held on to everything: my anger at Jesse for taking my place . . . and my hurt.

It was all I had.

I blamed Jesse for everything: my pain, my sadness, my broken dreams.

I blamed him and secretly hated myself because I couldn't let go of my anger . . . and because there was this place deep inside me that wanted life to be as it was before there ever was a Jesse.

I could see a brilliant prick of light piercing the darkness.

I could heard the whisper of wind gutting the shadow forest with a shuddering rumble.

Shadow leaves trembled, and silhouetted branches jerked about as the point of light grew at the center of a black onyx eye.

Coalescing about the shiny black orb, a long crystalline horse's head thrashed and gnashed its black teeth while its tormented tongue battled the rip of a crystal bit. Rearing upon its shimmering haunches, the stallion staggered blindly, its glittering mane flying from its arching neck as its silvery hooves raged at the curse of the distorted Red Prince preying on its back.

Rippling and rolling on a rearing luminescent gray quartz horse, half of the Orange Prince appeared behind his red brother. As the rest of him arrived, desperately hanging on to his blue crystal saddle, rows upon rows of black-and-silver-armored Basalt Guards slammed to attention behind him, their spears and spikes blasting yellow light.

Somehow I was watching the world of fossil shadows exploding back to life and the slithering shadow of a Raptor sinking its long teeth into the leg of a Soldier and sucking the light right out of him.

Attacking the Raptor, the Guards' incandescent spear tips barely bothered the glittering light of its newly charged body. The Raptor viciously snapped and slashed at them until one end of the Red Prince's sword shot from its handle and the scything tip pierced the Raptor's crackling skin.

Screeching as its light was sucked away, the Raptor shrank to a shadow.

As his Soldiers feasted on their recaptured light, the Red Prince wheeled on his frightened brother with a twisted grin. "This—this is where I want to beee!" he gloated.

"Oui! Zis is where yoo *should* be," the Orange Prince replied sourly, his ill-fitting crystal armor slipping off one shoulder.

"You want that you go back to your mama queen?" the Red Prince sneered, as fossil shadows swooped down on two Soldiers and pulled them screaming from the ranks. "BAASSALLT GUARDS!" he roared.

Ignoring their fallen comrades, the Soldiers saluted with a great stamping of feet.

The Orange Prince winced at the dying grind of the two Soldiers' screams, and the Red Prince brayed at his cowardly brother, "These are shadows! You are afraid of small shadows?"

"Een case yoo deedn't noteece," the Orange Prince quaked, "zey are feeding on our *light*, idiot." His chin wrenched at his neck, causing his orange battle helmet to go askew. "How do yoo know zat zee Humans are eefen here?" he challenged.

Slicing an attacking fossil in two, the Red Prince filled with more light and replied in delight, "We don't!"

"OUI!" the Orange Prince yelled as he tried to control his rearing mount. "An' how doo we know zat our light weel not be taken—poof?"

"Hah! We don't!" repeated the Red Prince, dispatching

another glittering fossil shadow. "Any time, any place, this maybe happins," he grinned, then playfully lunged at his brother. "Waatch out!" he shrieked in mock horror.

The Orange Prince spun so quickly, his helmet turned sideways.

Smirking at his brother's cowardice, the Red Prince sneered, "Make up your mind, leetle brather, or my Soldiers weell do it for you!"

Suddenly the tips of the Red Prince's double sword crackled and swelled with light.

The fossil shadows stopped attacking the Soldiers and began skittering in circles.

Its light streaking overhead, an Amber disappeared into the shadow trees. Another Amber shot past, and a third slowed to a stop and began vibrating high above the Red Prince's sword.

"Amberr aneemal!" whispered the Red Prince. "Off this I haf heard!"

Fascinated by a prehistoric wasp caught inside the vibrating Amber, the Red Prince raised one tip of his sword and painted a slow oval of light.

Mesmerized by the bright pulse of the scything tip, the Amber floated closer.

The Red Prince smiled. "It cannot help itself!" he giggled, barely able to contain his excitement.

Vibrating faster, the Amber Wasp inched even closer.

"Cahm leetle whan," the Red Prince whispered. "Cahm to me!"

The Red Prince's horse spooked and reared.

The Amber Wasp hesitated, and, in that moment, the Red Prince quickly spun the blade of his sword.

Darting at the sudden flare, the Amber Wasp exploded on the white-hot tip, and the Orange Prince nearly tumbled off his rearing horse as the Soldiers roared at the Amber's light rolling through them.

Lazily twirling his brilliantly rippling blades above his hideous crystal head, the Red Prince challenged the remaining Ambers to escape the lure of his incandescent sword.

"The Amber aneemals weell lead us!" he exulted, and his troops shivered in anticipation. "And they weell feed us!"

Wheeling around to face his men, he screamed, "Too tha liiight!"

"TO THA LIIIGHT!" his Soldiers roared back, "TO THA LIIIGHT!" and they stomped into a shattering march.

How did I know that the Red Prince was coming? How was I seeing this?

I had closed my eyes when we stopped to rest in the middle of a large cave that glinted brownish yellow from the Ambers' receding light. Suddenly I saw these hard crackling images of the Red Prince, the Orange Prince, their Soldiers, and horses in a furious battle with the fossils. Then to my amazement, I saw images of Jesse even though he was far behind me. I mean, I could *really* see him, as if I were with him, close enough to touch, and I could see the expression on his face as he resolutely stomped after me, his mouth open, yelling "Maggie!"

I didn't know what to do: wait for Jesse, or keep going.

In a panic, I opened my eyes, and there was Gneiss, holding on to a stalagmite, trying to speak.

I remembered studying stalagmites in school. They grew into upside-down icicle shaped things from dripping *stalactites* that hung from the ceiling above them. I liked geology. My science teacher liked to say that like socks and oxygen atoms, stalactites and stalagmites tended to come in pairs.

Gneiss waved his hand. "We gotta talk," he grunted. "Dere's somethin' I gotta ask ya."

"I don't have time to talk." I replied impatiently and stood up. There was no way I could prove to Jesse that I knew the Red Prince was coming. I had to find the Amber Girl. I had to get back to the Holy Clear before Jesse could talk her into moving him to the Land of Magma in his senseless need to find the supposed Wizard of Iz. I had to decide which tunnel to take.

"Why are we chasin' tha Ambers?" Gneiss wheezed. "I thought you hated those things. I mean, we don't really need them."

"Yes, we do," I reminded him. "They moved us through the petrified wall, right?"

"Yeah, okay . . ." he shrugged. "So?"

"So, they know *how* to move, right?" The tunnel on the left looked brighter. "What were you going to tell me?"

Gneiss looked surprised, like he hadn't thought of the Ambers' ability to move, then mumbled, "Nothin'. Nothin' that won't wait," and headed down the tunnel on the right.

I couldn't help myself, and closed my eyes for just for a moment.

The wind swirling about the Red Prince, and the fossil shadows were shrieking.

They swooped and stabbed at the fracturing spits and sprays of light that shot from the stamping feet of his crystal Soldiers, who kept marching in place, their stony faces inches from the petrified cliff face.

Forcing his black-eyed horse beneath the twisting branches, the Red Prince peered closely at the deep gouges that ran all the way to the top.

"Sahmthing iss heer!" he whispered insistently.

"Oui," whined the Orange Prince. "Zee Holy Clear was right: you suffer from zee mineral deficiency. It's a wall! A beeg wall zat goes forever wiz seengs steeckeeng out!" he cried, waving his arms about.

Ignoring his hysterical brother, the Red Prince touched one end of his sword to the rock surface. A flash of blue light ripped through him and his terrified horse, then surged through the ranks of his Soldiers.

The Orange Prince's cloudy steed crackled and screamed at the devouring light and nearly whirled away without him.

"They are neer!" the Red Prince exclaimed as he wrestled his twisting mount. "They are neer!" he screamed at his stunned Soldiers.

"NEER!" they roared, raising their crystal spears.

Hesitating, the Red Prince laid his sword back onto the wall and watched in awe as his arm became incandescent and disappeared into the gouged surface.

Twisting back to his Soldiers, he bellowed, "NOWW! NOWW!" and drove his crazed horse into the wall.

One second he was there, the next he was gone.

The Orange Prince and the Soldiers gazed amazedly at the white-hot hole through which he had vanished.

"Perhaps zere ees anozzer way," the Orange Prince suggested, trying to get control of his chin and neck. "I don' seenk eet ees posseeble for ever-ryone to fit into such a leetle—"

With a deafening roar the Soldiers surged forward, their spears and shields held high as they swept the Orange Prince and his terrified horse into the blinding light.

Jesse held Princess Amethyst by the arm as they struggled up a rocky slope toward two cave-like openings barely visible in the Ambers' dying afterglow. Her violet light had become a cloudy purple, and the following lights of Pyrope, Scheelite, and Torri had dimmed to dull. Pyrope was doing his best to support Scheelite, and Baz was carrying Torri piggyback, her arms wrapped tightly around his neck.

"So. You ah uh soldiuh?" Torri asked Baz, bravely trying to make conversation.

Baz grunted.

"How long have ya been a soldiuh. Do yuh lahk bein' a soldiuh?"

"I am Basalt GUAARD, number four-one-three-nine-two-SIX!" Baz answered, dutifully.

"Oh! That's such a nice numbah! An' you ah cuh-yoot as well," she said laying her weakly pulsing head on the back of his shoulder. "An' so strong—even if yuh ah so serious. Ah'm not holdin' on too taght, am ah? Ah we gettin' any closuh?" she asked, like a child waiting for Santa.

"We're stopping," Baz announced, gently lowering Torri to the ground.

They had arrived at the dimly glowing openings of the two tunnels.

Jesse helped the Princess sit as Pyrope helped Scheelite to the ground.

"So, if thuh ayuh is thuh 'heaven above,'" Torri whispered in the inky quiet, "an' Humans live in this heaven abuv, an' thuh paht of them that's in boxes is not who they really ah, then who ah they—really?"

"My mother says that we are all children of God," Jesse replied, anxiously peering into the dying afterglow in both tunnels. "We live in the air, and our heaven is everywhere."

"Heaven UP or heaven DOWN?" Baz asked.

"It's everywhere," Jesse replied, distracted.

"So you are the child of a god?" whispered the Princess.

I could hear Jesse's thoughts racing through his mind; why was I always so angry and mean to him . . . It wasn't his fault this had happened . . . Why had it happened . . . Did he want me to get lost . . . How could he even think that . . . Would I miss him . . . Would he ever see his mother again . . . Which tunnel should he take . . . What if he chose wrong? The questions piled one on top of the other, and I wondered if Jesse could see and hear me as well.

"What if Maggie gets lost?" asked Pyrope.

Torri weakly pointed from one tunnel to the other. "Eeny, meeny, mahny, moh, catch an Ahmbuh bah thuh toe—"

"If we don't choose SOON, there won't be any light to choose FROMM!" Baz observed brilliantly.

"What if it's the other one?" Scheelite quaked, trying to stand. She couldn't.

"We just cayn't lose thuh Ambuhs!" Torri exclaimed weakly, her colors barely flickering.

Watching Jesse struggle, Princess Amethyst whispered, "A choice is just a choice, Jesse. Not good or bad, not right or wrong. 'What if?' and 'What will happen?' don't make the choice. You do."

"Soon there will BEE no light," chimed in Baz. "SOON—"

"No!" Jesse cried, reaching into his pocket. "We have the flashlight! We can make light anytime—"

His face paled.

Frightened, he reached into his other pockets.

"It's gone!" he squeaked in disbelief.

"Gone?" echoed Pyrope.

"What's gone?" whispered Torri.

"How?" murmured Scheelite, her light surging dimly.

"I—I don't know how!" panicked Jesse, getting down on his knees and feeling around on the ground in the darkness. "I don't know! I lost it! Somehow I lost it! How did I lose it?"

"We haf tuh fahnd it," Torri's voice whispered from the darkness.

"Go-BAACK!" Baz instructed, his voice sounding detached, slower. "We go back—retrace . . . our . . . STEPS."

"In the dark?" Scheelite asked with little interest, her faint voice trailing off.

His battle-scarred face barely visible, Baz asked Jesse in a slow hollow whisper, "When did . . . you last h-o-l-L-D-IT?"

"I don't know," Jesse cried, searching frantically. "At the wall? When did anyone last see it?"

Nobody answered.

They couldn't.

Their light had gone out.

The Princess stood stock-still.

Baz was frozen in place like a statue, his arm extended.

Pyrope's silhouette knelt in a dim flicker beside a lightless Scheelite.

Torri sat motionless, staring out at nothing.

Jesse cried softly in the dark. His heart was broken, as

was the promise that he made to himself never, ever to lose faith—never to stop believing.

He hadn't said good-bye to Mom—or Dad, me or Cody. He'd never again see Molly or Blue—or the sun through his bedroom window, or his model planes floating above his bed.

They were all gone.

My Mirror—My Self

When Emily Zuba told me she didn't want to be my best friend anymore, I was devastated.

I refused to come out of my room for a whole day.

I sat on my bed and cried and my mother tried to console me, but I didn't want to be consoled. I wanted to never have a best friend ever again. I wanted Emily Zuba to fall down a well, and I wanted to be left alone.

Forever!

I didn't even care when Jesse invited himself into my room dragging his ratty old teddy bear. I let him climb onto my bed and watch me cry.

After a while I stopped, and we just sat there and listened to the rain.

Then Jesse took his wet, red, wrinkly thumb out of his mouth and held my hand.

Even though I could barely make out the shape of the flashlight in the dark, I knew right away what it was.

A horrible feeling came over me. "Jesse's fla—" I blurted in disbelief. "How did you—? When did you—?" My voice came echoing back from three more tunnel openings we had found.

"When we moved," Gneiss mumbled. "Troo da wall," he explained, avoiding my eyes. "Everytin' was floatin' around, ya know?" he asked, then shrugged. "So I grabbed it."

"Why didn't you say something?" I demanded angrily.

"I wanted tuh," insisted Gneiss. "I didn' know what ta do, ya know? Dere was da flishlight and den we were comin' outa da wall an' . . ." He shrugged. "I dunno."

"You could have said something! You could have told me!" I protested, feeling guilty.

Slowly nodding his head, Gneiss looked at me sideways. "Question: If I had said sometin' to ya, would y'have given it back to your brudda?" He raised his rock eyebrows and a small sprinkle of mica dusted his nose. "Den we'd *all* be goin' tuh da Land of Magma to look for the Wizard of Iz!"

No! I wasn't going to go where no one had ever been—to a place that these crystal people only believed existed. It made no sense!

"De Amber Girl likes ya," Gneiss observed, "or radder dere's sometin' in ya dat she likes, y'know? Da way she got lighter when she came closa to ya? For some reason, she wants, she needs your light, and, as you wuz sayin,' she knows how to *move.*"

I started to shake my head, and he held up a granite hand.

"Ya don' have to believe it's da 'de-enn-ay' stuff," he said pointedly. "You don' have to believe in anything, but when she gets close to ya, she makes more light. She can move us back ta da Kingdom, back ta da Holy Clear . . . who wants da *flishlight*."

He was right. Gneiss had said that he believed that the Holy Clear could move us home. With the flashlight, I could make light wherever I was, and as the Princess had said, when Metamorphos created light, it went everywhere all at once. So Jesse would never have to be in the dark, and I could come back and take him home.

"So—would ya have given it back?" Gneiss insisted.

I didn't know. Okay, I knew, even if I didn't want to admit it. However, the Red Prince was coming and we were running out of time.

"We got da flishlight," Gneiss gently reasoned, holding it up for me. "We can't change dat. Da question is, what's best fuh all—fuh everyone?"

I took it.

The metal surface was cold and hard, and it was heavier than I remembered.

"Toin it on," Gneiss whispered.

I closed my eyes.

In a great crackling and rippling of light, the Red Prince's horse was backing out of the massive opal wall, its front hooves flailing in terror at the brilliant wash of colors as the Orange Prince and the broken ranks of Soldiers stumbled out behind them in confusion.

Raising his awful twin-bladed sword, the Red Prince yanked on his mount's crystal reins and viciously twisted its wild-eyed head onto its flank.

Wheeling about, he bellowed, "MAKE RANKS!"

Suddenly, the white of the sudden light storm from Jesse's flashlight ripped through the gathered Soldiers.

Caught in confusion, they froze in the blast of light.

The Orange Prince shook as if he were being electrocuted.

Then it was gone.

Men and horses stood dazed, staring at a curtain of amber orbs vibrating violently before them.

The Red Prince couldn't speak, and his arm rattled with light as he slowly pointed his white-hot weapon at the Ambers.

Instantly they shot off in different directions.

"YIELD!" bellowed the Red Prince.

Some Ambers slowed.

"I say, yield!" he screamed. "Yield! YIELLLD!"

They couldn't resist the light of his sword. Still vibrating, the Ambers formed a constellation of lights high above the Red Prince and his Soldiers.

Smiling hungrily, the Red Prince gloated. "Look at thiis—thiis liight!" he cried.

Then he pointed to the remaining flashes of light storming on the horizon and shouted victoriously, "And look—there! AT THAAT LIIGHT!"

Jesse recoiled in amazement from the blinding storm.

Baz's frozen face twitched.

Scheelite's hand jumped.

Torri's pale green eyes snapped open, and a violet glow blossomed deep inside the Princess as Pyrope ignited white and the crashing light enveloped them in a deafening roar.

Gneiss was trying to blink away a riot of white spots. "We got light! We got da light!" he yelped. "Ya see? We can return ta King Bloo and da Kingdom of Beryl! We can go anywhere we like!"

At last I had the flashlight, and there was no more darkness!

We were standing in a landscape of vast canyons, and I felt giddy, as if I were floating on currents of energy.

Maggie-me, Maggie-me,

Come-to-me-now . . .

The Amber Girl's whisper echoed all around us.

I turned around and there she was, floating in front of her brilliant cloud of amber orbs.

Rotating forward as if she were bowing, she backed away from us.

Come-to-me-Maggie,

Let-us-see-now;

Your-light-is-within-us,

Let-us-see-how.

Her orb rose higher and the Ambers parted, revealing a barely glowing, scrawny shape lying on the ground beneath her.

It was a small Christmas tree!

Its naked opal branches pulsed with dim light as the luminescent insect Ambers floated up to them. For the briefest moment, the branches would blossom with tiny opal rainbows that quickly vanished as the spent Ambers fell lightless to the ground.

More waves of Ambers kept floating up to the petrified tree, giving their light, then dying, while the clicks and whines of the other Ambers grew into a great humming that sounded like the inside of an angry beehive.

Come-to-me-Maggie,

Come-to-me-now.

Your-light-is-within-us,

Light-our-tree-now.

"What's dat?" asked Gneiss, pointing at the fallen fir.

"It's a tree!" I whispered in awe. "A Christmas tree!"

The Amber Girl's voice sang higher.

Come-to-me-Maggie,

To-the-tree-come,

To-the-tree, light-the-tree,

Light-the-tree-come . . .

Pulling at my arm, Gneiss urgently whispered, "Da tree ting's losin' its light! She wants you ta give it more light!"

I looked at the naked tree, and a wave of sadness came over me. I wished that I hadn't left Jesse, and I wished that I wasn't such a disappointment to my mother. I wished that none of this had happened and that I could go back and make everything all right.

"Da Amber Girl can move!" Gneiss reminded me. He waved a stone hand at her. "If we give da tree da light, can ya move us to da Kingdom of Beryl?" he asked eagerly.

To-the-tree, light-a-me,

Light-the-tree come—

"Hold on, hold on," Gneiss interrupted, shaking his head. "Only if ya help us move," he negotiated.

Come-a-me, to-the-tree—

"NO!" I cried at the Amber Girl. "No! You know how to move. We know you can move!"

In-a-tree, in-a-tree,

Part-of-me-see.

Sap-of-me

In-a-tree,

In-a-tree-me—

"Stop!" I shouted. "If you want me to light your tree, you have to help us move!"

"She can't," replied Jesse's angry voice.

He was standing between Princess Amethyst and Pyrope, alongside Scheelite, Torri, and Baz. They were all watching me with expressions of hurt and disapproval.

"She can't," he repeated quietly, "because that petrified Christmas tree once had sap that was alive, just as the girl was once alive. She knows that sap, Maggie, because she's been preserved in it. She remembers being alive. She can't leave the tree. She can't leave her own life!" He held out his hand. "You stole my flashlight. Give it back to me!"

"I didn't steal your stupid flashlight! How do you know what she remembers, or that she can't leave her sap or her tree?" I demanded.

He started toward me. "Give it to me, Maggie," he insisted grimly.

"No way! I am not going to any Land of Magma!" I cried.

The Amber Girl kept singing:

In-the-tree-come . . .

Light-a-me-some,

In-the-tree light-a-me,

Light-a-me-some.

"What is a Christmas tree?" asked Scheelite.

Stalking me, Jesse answered her: "My mother says it's a tree we decorate with light in order to bring back light." I was still six inches taller than Jesse, but he didn't look as if he cared.

"Give me back my flashlight . . . Maggie!"

"How duz the tree bring back the laaght?" Torri asked, confused.

"It doesn't; we do, with our prayers." Jesse answered, stopping in front of me, his grimy paw waiting for his flashlight.

In-the-tree light-a-me,

Light-a-me-some . . .

Jesse grabbed for the flashlight.

"Forget it!" I spat, jumping back. "You haven't got a chance!"

"Give it to me, Maggot," Jesse warned, his jaw clenched, his chin trembling. "Last chance."

"Forget it!" I snorted, backing away. "Finders keepers, losers weepers."

"You can't go back to the Kingdom of Beryl, jerk!" he cried. "There's nothing there."

"Well, there's nothing in the Land of Magma, either!" I argued.

Jesse lunged and got his hand on the flashlight.

"That's mine!" he cried.

I twisted away, and he fell.

"Not anymore it isn't!" I replied.

Picking up a rock, he scrambled to his feet with an ugly look on his face. "Give it to me, Maggie," he demanded threateningly.

"Jesse!" gasped the Princess.

There was a sharp jolt, and the ground convulsed.

We froze.

"What was that?" whispered Scheelite.

"Its da great crushin'!" blurted Gneiss.

"It's thuh great carusshin'!" repeated Torri.

There was a second jolt and something fell from above, nearly hitting me.

It was a rectangular piece of metal . . .with writing on it. Was I seeing things? An old street sign was lying at my feet!

I looked up.

In the glow of the Ambers, a dim shape hung high above us where great rock walls had converged to form the roof of a canyon.

It seemed to be . . . it seemed to be the front of an old streetcar suspended nose first from the top of the canyon wall! It looked about to come crashing down at any second.

Near it, a street lamp hung from a ribbon of concrete that was turned onto its side and disappeared up into a maze of broken pipes of all different lengths and sizes that were protruding like amputated fingers from a roof of rocks and dirt. Twisted steel beams stuck out of large torn chunks of concrete, and the hulk of an antique steam shovel, its lower jaw hanging from a corner of its gaping metal mouth, rested on the rusty roof of an old bulldozer.

"Look!" Jesse gasped. "We must be under the ruins of a city!"

"A 'city'?" parroted Pyrope.

"Oh my God! . . . Oh my God!" I sputtered. "That's where we come from! Up there!" I cried, pointing past the rocky slopes to the bowels of the city. "There are people, trees, cars, buildings—"

"Cars . . . ? BILLdings . . . ?" Baz grunted, staring above him.

Pointing at a hairy weave of twisted roots reaching through the tangle of pipes, Gneiss asked nervously "What's dat?"

"Roots!" exclaimed Jesse. "They're part of trees—live trees!"

"Christmas trees?" asked Scheelite.

I started to climb. I didn't know how I was going to get up there, but I didn't care.

"All kinds of trees!" Jesse replied and began climbing as well.

"Hold on," Gneiss called as he climbed after me.

The others followed, and the Amber Girl sang after us:

> *Light-a-me,*
>
> *Light-a-me,*
>
> *In-a-tree-come . . .*
>
> *In-a-tree light-a-me,*
>
> *Light-a-me-some.*

I climbed faster.

"We can go home!" I cried.

"Go where?" Pyrope called out as he helped Scheelite over a crumbling brick wall.

Stepping between old green and brown broken glass bottles that were sticking out of oily black sand, I scraped my hand on a rotted pipe that was green with corrosion, but I couldn't stop.

"Help!" yelled Gneiss. He had lost his footing and was tumbling back down to the others. They had all stopped climbing and were just standing there staring up at the strange world above them.

"Come on!" I called as Gneiss hurriedly pulled himself to his feet and started climbing again.

"Wait for me! Hold on!" he cried, clawing his way over a pile of old bricks.

The Princess held up her hands. "We don't know the air above," she replied. "We don't know 'up there.' We can't move up there."

"But we have light!" I yelled impatiently. I pointed up at the bottom of the city. "And you can see it. You can see 'up there'! Just look!"

Shaking his head in confusion, Pyrope mumbled, "I just see 'roots' and those other things."

"We can't go up there, Maggie," Jesse replied.

"Why not?" I demanded. "We can try. We can at least try!"

"Maggie! Give me the flashlight!" he demanded.

"No!" I cried and continued climbing.

The Amber Girl kept singing.

Maggie-me, Maggie-me,

Light-a-me-now,

In-the-tree

Light-a-me,

Light-a-me-now.

"You're dead!" I yelled down at her, and I scrambled for the streetcar. "The tree's dead. I'm alive!"

CRAAACK! There was another really big jolt. A shower of gravel rained down on me, and Gneiss lost his balance and rolled back down.

The ground shifted, and there was a sudden gust of hot wind.

The lights of the Ambers momentarily dulled.

"Uh-ohhh . . ." muttered Baz.

Vibrating violently, two of the Ambers darted away, and a third shot off in another direction.

The first two disappeared behind a cliff, and two explosions of light were followed by a third from somewhere behind us.

"Oh maah!" Torri cried in alarm.

Two more Ambers streaked away, while the others protectively crowded around their scrawny Christmas tree, clicking and humming louder.

Appearing from behind the distant rock formation, the Red Prince held his incandescent sword high above his prancing steed as he led his marching Soldiers toward us.

The two streaking Ambers collided with his sword, and his Soldiers roared in the shower of light.

"Dis is jus' terrific!" muttered Gneiss, as Torri helped him up off the ground.

More Ambers abandoned the Christmas tree, and the hum of the others grew into a high whine.

"I think we better reTREAT," suggested Baz.

Yelling up to me, Jesse cried, "Maggie! We've gotta go to the Land of Magma! Give me the flashlight!"

He reached out to the Amber Girl and pleaded, "You've gotta help us, please! We need to find Metamorphos. We need to find the source of light!"

"What are we going to do?" asked Scheelite, panicking.

"Look!" cried Pyrope, pointing to a high ridge behind us.

Surrounded by his massing Soldiers, the Orange Prince reared on his glittering horse as two more Ambers exploded on his spear. Giggling in delight, he bubbled deliciously until his Soldiers roared and plunged over the ridge, carrying him and his horse riding down an avalanche of dust.

Gneiss was beside himself. "De're eatin' da Ambuhs!" he yelled. "An' dey'll eat us when de're done!"

The Amber Girl's light was pulsing more rapidly as the clicks and cries of the smaller Ambers got louder.

Jesse implored her, "Look at me! Look at me! Please! We are alive. We're all alive! You can help us . . ."

Bowing, the Amber Girl backed into her cloud of Ambers as Jesse ran after her.

"No! Please—" he begged, and the entire cloud was instantly sucked through a pinhole of light, which blinked and then disappeared.

The Amber Girl was gone.

Loss

When we were little and I wanted to really scare Jesse, I'd tell him I was going to take him somewhere and leave him.

Then I lost him at the mall. Suddenly he was gone and I couldn't find him anywhere.

In a panic, I ran into the last store that Mom had gone into, but she wasn't there. I couldn't find her either.

I had never felt so alone.

Eyes squeezed shut, the Orange Prince desperately held onto his screaming steed's neck as it lunged up a steep slope after Scheelite and Pyrope.

Gneiss had grabbed Torri and they had managed to reach the hanging streetcar. As he lowered her into the cavernous metal shell, she stepped on a row of dead batteries and watched in horror as a film of white corrosion instantly climbed up her body.

"Help! Somebo—" she screamed, her voice and light drowning under the swarming white.

"Hey! Get offa her!" cried Gneiss, but no matter how much he brushed it away, more came back until it had covered them both.

Reaching down from a narrow ledge of crumbling bricks, Jesse grabbed the Princess's hand just as a Soldier attacked Baz from behind.

"BAZ!" Jesse screamed.

Dodging the deadly spear, Baz grabbed hold of the shaft and leapt high into a twisting somersault over the Soldier's head.

The Soldier held on to his weapon, his upraised arms contorting into a knot as the spear came full circle and pierced his back. He roared his pain as his light drained from him and surged through Baz, who flashed a brilliant yellow and landed on his feet facing three more Soldiers.

"BAZ! . . . BAZ!" Jesse yelled, pulling the Princess on to the ledge. "MY HAND—Take my hand!"

In a blur, Baz dispatched the three Soldiers.

Three more took their place.

Running for the ledge, he caught Jesse's hand and tried to climb.

Wincing from the pain of Baz's crushing grip, Jesse tried to hang on, but his arm felt as if it were going to rip off.

"Baz!" Jesse screamed as the faithful Guard's hand slipped from his fingers.

Covered in corrosion, Gneiss and Torri clung to the hanging streetcar as a rattling shake separated it from its rock ledge.

Suddenly, the huge container was sliding!

With a roar of screaming steel and falling rock, it plunged nose first into a rock ledge that was swarming with Soldiers.

Stunned, Gneiss and Torri tried to get their bearings as the Soldiers began banging their spears on the metal walls and thrusting the white-hot tips through the broken windows.

Pushing Torri as far as he could from the twisted openings, Gneiss tried to distract the Soldiers by climbing down toward the front of the streetcar.

A blazing spear stabbed past his nose.

Flattening himself against a rusted wall, he spied a Soldier crawling through a broken window above Torri.

More Soldiers were coming through the other openings.

Torri screamed as Gneiss struggled to climb back up to where she was.

The first Soldier beat him to her.

Gneiss reached up for Torri, and the Soldier's spear caught him squarely on his corroded chest.

To his and the Soldier's amazement, the white layer of powder ate the spear's light, and the smothering crust shattered into small pieces.

Grabbing hold of the spear, Gneiss pulled down on it with all his might, and the stunned Soldier fell screaming onto his comrades below.

My legs felt heavier than lead.

"Climb! Climb, Maggie! C'mon—climb!" I kept yelling at myself, but I couldn't take another step. The Soldiers were upon us.

I could see Pyrope holding Scheelite close to him in a tangled patch of barbed wire. The Orange Prince sat smugly on his horse a short distance away and watched his soldiers surround them. He smiled and waved at Scheelite and then commanded his Soldiers to extract her and Pyrope.

There was Jesse! He was scrambling over a collapsed roof, screaming for Baz, who had disappeared in a broil of fighting soldiers.

Turning back to help the Princess, Jesse froze.

Behind her, the Red Prince sat on his flashing horse, a twisted smile splitting his misshapen face.

"You think you arr getting away?" he sneered, approaching Jesse on his skittish steed. "Too sooon, too soon. We talk about za flashlight, dah?"

Another tremor rolled through the ground knocking Jesse to his knees.

Loss

The Red Prince's horse reared in panic, its hooves stabbing at Jesse.

"NO!" screamed the Princess.

Suddenly, the Prince folded sharply to one side, as a brilliant shower of light spewed from his body.

Holding on to the other end of a crackling spear, Baz stood behind the Red Prince, stunned by the surging infusion of light.

The Prince's darkening horse crumpled to its knees and the Red Prince started to spasm and shake. Grimacing in agony, he strained to lift the stone handle of his sword as Baz shuddered uncontrollably, unable to let go of the still-surging spear.

Seething against the drowning darkness, the Red Prince screamed and squeezed the handle until splinters of fiery red light spat from the fracturing knuckles of his crackling fist.

The opposing tips of the Red Prince's blades pulsed brighter, and the light boiled up his arm into his massive chest and filled his fallen horse. Then came another wave, and another. The Red Prince was willing himself back to light!

Suddenly Baz's spear flew off the Prince's crystal body in an explosion of light.

Baz kept his grip on the weapon, braced himself, and swung the glowing tip back toward the Red Prince, who had forced his reviving steed up onto its hind legs and wheeled to counter Baz's attack.

CRRAAACK!

With a booming roar, the ground suddenly lifted, and the Red Prince and his horse were carried ten feet to their right.

Dodging the Prince's staggering mount, Baz attempted to reach Princess Amethyst.

"HooooOOld! HOOLLDD!" he yelled to her as she struggled to keep her feet.

BOOM!

With a thunderous roar the ground tore apart, and, amid a great shower of rocks, a massive ledge rose up with a deafening rumble. Sliding overhead, it separated us from the bowels of the city.

"It's da crushin'!" screamed Gneiss, falling away from Torri with a look of surprise.

Screaming for his brother, the Orange Prince was spun in a circle by his hysterical horse as an entire flank of Soldiers vanished.

Everything was a darkening blur of falling rock and explosions of dust . . . and then it just stopped.

There was nothing.

No light.

No sound.

Just silence.

Loss

What had happened?

I couldn't move.

I couldn't see.

Where was I? Where were the others?

I was buried to my neck, and I could barely breathe. My heart throbbed painfully in my ears.

I could feel the flashlight still clutched in my hand, but the earth held me tight.

Where was Jesse? I closed my eyes and tried to see him . . . to hear him, but now I couldn't.

"Oh God," I pleaded, "please don't let us die! Please make this all a bad dream. I want my baby brother. I want to see Mommy and Daddy and Molly and Blue, and I'm sorry, so sorry, for what I've done. Please! Please! I don't want to die!"

A small sliver of light shot from the earth.

It became two, three, four thin shafts—then a burst of light.

His mica flashing, Baz climbed out of the ground and, with a grunt, pulled Torri out after him.

She was desperately clinging to Gneiss's hand.

Whispering gently to him, she helped him up. "Cuhm on then; that's right. Cuhm on . . . we ah heah, we ah all raght."

"Here! Over here!" I yelled. "Help me!"

Baz and the others rushed over and began digging me out.

"Where's Jesse?" I demanded. "Where's—?"

Everybody started hollering for Jesse.

"No! Stop!" I cried. "*Listen!* Listen for him."

"Princess Ame-THYSST?" Baz called into the surrounding darkness. "Prin-CESSSS?"

Standing at the very edge of our circle of light, he waited for her answer.

All we heard was silence.

There was a small jolt, and rocks started falling.

"Uh oh," muttered Gneiss.

"Jesse . . . ! Jesse . . . !" I called, climbing out of the ground.

There was a muffled cry.

We listened for what seemed forever.

There it was again!

Baz took three steps, knelt, and drove his massive fist into the ground. He came up empty and thrust it into the earth again and again.

The cry came from behind him.

Wheeling about, he reached into the earth and pulled out Scheelite, her thin yellow arms clinging to Pyrope, who was unconscious, his dim light pulsing weakly.

Baz tried to separate Pyrope from Scheelite, but she wouldn't let go.

"Is he alahve?" whispered Torri.

"Pyrope? . . . Pyrope!" Scheelite called to him.

Pyrope didn't move.

"We have to help him!" Scheelite pleaded with me. "Please! Please give him some light! Give us your light."

"Hold it, hold it!" interrupted Gneiss fearfully. "What if da light brings back Red an' his Soldiers?"

"He's got a POINT," Baz grunted.

The Red Prince! Where was he? A chaos of images flashed before me. I had to find Jesse!

"JESSE!" I screamed into the darkness.

"Yuh have tuh give Pahrope sum laaght! Yuh haff tuh!" Torri insisted.

"Maybe Jesse needs the light too!" Scheelite cried. "Maybe it'll help find him!"

"If he is able too SEEE-iit," Baz had to add.

Nodding, Gneiss leaned into me. "Dere's somethin' else," he urged quietly. "Unless I'm mistaken, dere's no one else here dat knows how to move . . . except Pyrope. So, unless we want to spend da rest of eternity here . . ."

He was right. Turning on the light would help Pyrope and help Jesse if he was still—he was still, you know . . . okay. We needed Pyrope to get us out of there.

"Okay," I agreed. "Just for a second." I slid back the ring on Jesse's flashlight and was about to turn it on when a dim streak of light flashed past and disappeared.

There was another, and another.

"The Ambuhs!" whispered Torri.

Hovering above us, they seemed to have trouble floating. Their light was so dull you could hardly see the bugs inside them.

"They want the light!" squeaked Scheelite.

"Okay, already!" I said, relenting and holding up the flashlight. "Here!"

"Wait—wait!" Gneiss interrupted. "Dat's not da kind of light dey want. They want your other light, your DNA light."

Two of the Ambers hesitated, came closer, then shot away.

"Let them come. Let them come closer," the Princess whispered.

Remembering how skittish Molly and Blue were as colts, I held out my hand as if I had a lump of sugar.

"Come hea now, little Ambuhs, cuhm to thuh pritty lady," Torri cooed softly.

The Amber Wasp inched closer.

Following hesitantly, the others floated closer as well and started to glow.

"Oh mah! Oh mah!" Torri exclaimed.

Gently nudging and pushing against me, they kept getting brighter, and I could feel myself getting warmer and warmer.

Scheelite's light grew, and Pyrope stirred in her arms.

Torri shivered, and Gneiss began scratching at his blotches of mica.

"How do we toin it off," Gneiss asked nervously, "ya know, when we got enuff? We don' want dis goin' on too long."

BOOM!

There was a blast of wind, and rocks and dirt were flying everywhere.

Knocked to my knees, I struggled to climb back on my feet as beams of light reached through a cloud of dust that had engulfed us.

Immediately flying into the beams, two of the Ambers disintegrated in brilliant flashes.

Silhouetted by the blasting brightness, the Red Prince spurred his spooked horse through the swirling dust. Shivering with light, it snapped up its flashing hooves, carrying its master toward us in a slow sideways prance as the Orange Prince and the Soldiers surged through the gaping hole behind them.

Painfully poking me, Gneiss was whispering something, but I couldn't hear him. He pointed at the flashlight.

The flashlight!

I tried to hide it, but I couldn't find my pocket! Putting it behind my back, I couldn't take my eyes off the Red Prince's grotesque head as it slowly turned to me and fixed me with an ugly stare. It felt as if he were looking right through me.

He raised his horrible sword, and his Soldiers stamped to attention.

Dismounting, he slowly dragged his misshapen body toward me, and I shut my eyes.

A faint line of light was creeping up the blackness behind my eyelids.

It shifted, breaking into pieces.

I watched it slowly move up a pile of lightless white crystals then climb past dark angular shapes. Gently, it washed over the motionless face of Princess Amethyst.

Floating inches from the Princess's unseeing eyes, the Amber Girl waited for the Princess to waken, but her amethyst crystals remained dark and cloudy.

Rotating forward, the Amber Girl stared blindly toward the ground ... then slowly backed away from the Princess.

Her dim orb's ragged surface brushed over bumps and ridges, leaving small puffs of dust in its path, till it rolled into a small crevice ... quietly rocked back and forth ... then stopped and lay perfectly still as the trailing dust gently settled onto the orb's dull surface.

The frozen form of the Amber Girl began to disappear inside the darkening sphere.

Nearby, a single grain of crystal dislodged from a spiny ridge and tumbled down a steep slope.

A few more grains were shaken loose and chased the first.

At the base of the slope, a small split filled with more cascading grains, and then the overflowing fissure collapsed into a wider hole that swallowed the growing avalanche of tiny crystals in one gulp.

A finger poked through the piling grains.

There was another finger and another, and then Jesse's hand burst forth, followed by his arm and shoulder and finally his face, his mouth agape, gasping for air. He was alive! My brother was alive!

Wiping the dirt from his eyes, Jesse squinted up at the dim outline of the Amber Girl's outstretched hand, barely visible inside her dark orb.

He strained to touch the dull surface. "Please . . . don't!" he whispered. "Please, don't die!"

His shaking fingertips fell short, and he beat his fists against the earth that held him too close. Trying again and again, he finally collapsed beneath her motionless hand and wept.

He wept for mom and dad, and me, and all those he would never see again.

He didn't notice the pulse of light growing brighter in her chest.

It was the wave of warmth kissing the back of his neck that caused him to look up.

The Amber Girl's eyes were filling with light, and her glowing orb was slowly rising off the ground.

Pulsing brighter and brighter, she floated higher as shadows twisted and grew.

Igniting the white quartz at the bottom of the Princess's gown, the light steadily climbed up her dim, still figure till it filled her lifeless face.

Her amethyst eyes blinked open.

She looked at Jesse—and smiled.

I opened my eyes.

The Soldiers had surrounded us, their marching feet shaking the ground into a circle of dust that was skewered by the streaks of yellow light spitting from their spears.

Leaning to one side from his wound, the Red Prince held his

scything blade an inch above Baz's kneeling figure and raised his claw of a hand.

The marching ceased.

"Where is brother and Amethyst Princess?" he rasped angrily at Baz's bowed head. Gneiss shakily cleared his throat and began mumbling, "Dey, uh, said somethin' about da Land of Magma. Den we got separat'd, and—"

Swinging the slicing end of his sword, the Red Prince roared, "THAA LLIIGHT!"

Gneiss ducked just in the nick of time.

"We don't have it!" I blurted.

"We don' have it!" Torri screamed, her colors going all over the place.

"Mais non, Mademoiselle Toormaleene," the Orange Prince argued, his chin yanking his face in small circles, "weeth zee eyes wee haf seen eet!" Then he leaned into Scheelite with a throaty whisper and crooned, "Ma chère, eef yoo geef us zee light, zen nobody will get, yoo know . . . hurt."

"It mighta been da light from da Ambers ya saw," Gneiss quickly offered. "Y'know, when da boy turned on his flishlight?"

The Orange Prince was stumped by that piece of information.

The Red Prince pushed his big grotesque face to within an inch of mine. He smelled of rotting eggs, and his voice sounded like grating glass.

"Sahmthing . . . you hav sahmthing," he hissed insistently. "I can feel this. I can see in your eye."

I held his horrible stare. What could he see? What did he know?

"DEE-EN-AAY!" Baz blurted, trying to distract the Red Prince.

"What?" the Prince demanded, wheeling on him.

Baz fixed his gaze on Gneiss and repeated very clearly, "Dee-en-AAY—he feels Dee-en-AAY, RIGHT?"

The Red Prince examined Baz closely. He wasn't about to be fooled again. "You want that I ask about this dee-en-ay? Yah?" he observed, impressed by his own perceptiveness. "I am not stoopid!" he barked.

"Dat's it!" Gneiss blurted. "It's really all about da information—DNA, dat is. DNA is information. See, rocks don't have it; DNA, that is. However, we do have light, and it feels like information, but it's another kinda information," he concluded with a twitch.

The Red Prince stared in confusion at Gneiss and then jabbed the scything tip of his sword at Baz and changed the subject.

"Za Princess, she is your charge! Where is she?" he demanded.

Baz lowered his head in shame. "I do not know," he whispered.

The incandescent point of the Red Prince's sword lingered above Baz's head. "Then yoo arr not doing yoorr dutee and yoo will be shatterrred!" he sneered.

"As you WIILLL," Baz replied.

Scheelite gasped.

"NO!" cried Torri, her colors bursting.

"Then where is your light?" the Red Prince snarled impatiently.

"OUR LAGHT IS RAGHT HEAH!" Torri cried out.

My heart jumped into my throat. Torri was going to give up the flashlight?

"Where?" the Red Prince demanded.

"Raght heah!" Torri replied, standing up to the Red Prince and tapping her chest. "Insahd us!"

I could hear the rattle of Gneiss praying under his breath.

Staring at Torri as though he hadn't heard her correctly, the Red Prince was about to say something when the Orange Prince held up a ring-bedecked finger and prepared to speak, but before he could say a word, Baz interrupted him.

"The PRINCESS and the Jesse arr—"

The Red Prince dropped the tip of his sword on Baz's head, and a shattering blast of light ripped through us.

A soft cry died in Torri's throat as we gazed in horror at what was left of Baz—a pile of dust at the Red Prince's feet.

Sighing, the Red Prince smirked. "I should perhaps haf let him finish." Then he grinned. "Now, my sister za Priincess and za Jesse arr where?"

"Why did you do that?" I screamed. "You killed him! You, you—"

"Yesss I did, didn't I?" the Red Prince replied with a nasty smile.

"Yuh had no raght!" Torri cried, her chest turning deep red as her face broke into a thousand crackling colors. "Whut did he evah do tuh you? He wuz ah kahnd an' gentuhl Guahd!"

"We don't know where they are," Pyrope quietly insisted, staring at Baz's remains. "We parted in the crushing."

Her colors flashing angrily, Torri marched over to the Red Prince. "We don' have thuh slahtest ahdea if thuh Princess an' Jesse ah even alahve," she cried and pointed at Baz's remains. "An' neithuh did he when yuh—"

Ignoring Torri, the Red Prince brought the pulsing tip of his sword so close to my eye that I could barely see his horrid face through the glare. "Sahmthing is here!" he insisted.

I held my breath.

"You arr hiding this sahmthing, dah?" he asked with a crooked smile. "So. Who do I ask now?" The scything point wandered over to Scheelite. "'You think she knows?"

My eyes filled and I started to cry.

Watching my tears with curiosity, he whispered, "Aah, what is this? Water comink out of a goddess?"

He took a step toward Scheelite, and both tips of his double sword suddenly surged with light.

Stopping, the Red Prince stared at the pulsing points.

His face twitched, and he held himself very still as if he were trying to hear something.

"Take them to Beryl Kingdom," he abruptly commanded his brother.

Caught completely off guard, the Orange Prince stuttered, "P-pardonne? W-what are yoo—?"

"Za Jesse brather is alive," the Red Prince stated.

I closed my eyes. He knew. What could I do? Should I give him the flashlight? Would that save Jesse?

"He ees alive?" the Orange Prince echoed in surprise.

Holding up his glowing sword, the Red Prince gloated victoriously. "Light happins sahmwhere! He is alive, and he will try to find za sister. He will cahm with light!"

"He's alahve?" whispered Torri.

The Orange Prince wasn't so sure. "Un moment, s'il vous plaît," he interrupted. "Eefen supposeeng zee bruzzer ees a-life, what eef he duzzn't return to zee Keengdom of Beryl?" he pointed out, then winked confidently at Scheelite. "Hmmm?"

Sighing impatiently, the Red Prince explained as if to a three-year-old, "Use yourr too small hedd, idiot! This means I find him before he finds hurr!"

"I haf une questionne . . ." the Orange Prince argued.

" . . . Or," continued the Red Prince, his sword surging even brighter, "if you don' trahst me with light"—he sneered, pointing the blistering tip at Scheelite—"we destrroy prritty yellow thing and rest of these pipple right heer, right now," he offered with a nasty smile. "An' you, brave little orange brahther with head like teensy creestal, can cahm with!"

"MAGGIE!"

I could hear Jesse's echo die into the darkness.

"MAGGIE . . . ?" he called again, and I could hear the Amber Girl singing softly.

Alive-a-me, in-a-me,

Alone-I-see-how.

Alone-in-me,

See-in-me,

Be-in-me-now.

"Where's my sister?" Jesse demanded of the princess.

"We don't know," the Princess answered, her light pulsing quietly.

"Okay. So we'll find out!" Jesse insisted. "You know all about this stuff. Think. Think really hard! There's gotta be a way! We gotta find her. We gotta—"

"*We don't know, Jesse,*" the Princess repeated.

The Amber Girl drifted closer.

> *Alone-I-see,*
>
> *You-are-me,*
>
> *Help-a-you-now.*
>
> *Help-a-me,*
>
> *Help-a-you,*
>
> *Be-in-me-now.*

"I don't understand you!" he cried.

"She's singing about being alive, Jesse," the Princess explained gently. "She's singing about being alone."

"That's no help!" Jesse complained angrily.

"She's saying she'll help," replied the Princess.

Wheeling on the Amber Girl, Jesse demanded, "Who are you?"

The large amber orb rotated forward, and the Girl seemed to bow to him.

> *Life-in-me-kept-in-me,*

In-amber-me-how.

Keep-and-collect,

Of-memory-now.

"No!" Jesse challenged, opening and closing his fists in frustration. "Who are you!"

"The light reminds her of who she is. It reminds her that she existed before," explained the Princess, "even before she was human. She wants to go back, Jesse; she wants to go back to her 'knowing' of everything. She wants to help find the source of light—to find the God-Wizard."

Jesse shook his head. "No! I can't! Not without Maggie," he declared adamantly. "What if there is no God-Wizard? Or if there is, what if he doesn't have the secret of the source of light? And even if he does, if I can't find Maggie, if I can't find my sister—"

"Then you can't," the Princess gently stopped him. "Then you can't."

The finality of it all was too much for Jesse. His chin started to tremble.

"How will you know if you don't try?" whispered Princess Amethyst.

The Amber Girl pulsed before him.

Hear-in-me-Jesse,

Hear-in-me-how,

Fears-are-like-dragons

Inside-of-you-now,

Guarding-your-deepest-treasures,

See-in-me-how!

"What does that mean?" Jesse exclaimed angrily. "I don't know what 'dragons' and 'fears' and 'treasures' mean!"

"You will learn," assured the Princess. "You will remember those words, and you will learn."

Jesse's chest heaved and he tried not to cry, but this was all too much for him. "How? How do you know that I will learn?" he demanded, tears streaming down his cheeks.

"Think, Jesse . . . think!" the Princess whispered softly. "What would your mother do?"

IGNEUS THE NTH & THE GOD-WIZARD

Mom always talks about faith and hope.

She says that faith is the remembered experience of belonging to something bigger than you, of loving and being loved.

She says that hope is the memory of that experience, and belief is our faith that we can remember.

Why can't I remember?

Jesse and the Princess were staring up at an orange-and-black sky of tumbling cubes and rolling, pyramid-shaped clouds.

Steaming black mesas dotted a burning horizon across a jigsaw puzzle of flat and barren plains that were chopped into thousands of pieces by fiery fissures, spitting splashes of orange hot magma from their jagged cracks.

"This is the Land of Magma!" Jesse whispered in awe.

Three glowing Ambers—a Dragonfly, a Wasp, and a Butterfly—floated above them.

Jesse searched for the Amber Girl. "Where is she?" he asked, confused.

"The Amber Girl couldn't leave her tree," replied the Princess, "so she gave us her light."

"No!" cried Jesse.

"She couldn't, Jesse," the Princess reminded him. "You said so yourself."

Jesse didn't want to believe he might never see the Amber Girl again. "But we moved! How did we—?"

"*I* moved. With her light," the Princess replied and indicated the three Ambers. "She sent these in her place."

"But . . . but if she has no light, how will she survive?" Jesse asked.

Nodding, the Princess explained gently, "That's what she wanted."

"I'll never see her again," Jesse whispered, trying to understand the finality of it all.

"It depends on where you need to find her," the Princess offered. "You'll always have the memory of her."

Searching the vast plains, Jesse cried, "But where do we go? How do we find—?" He stopped and stared in shock.

A giant funnel of dust was moving toward them from across the cracked plains. Beneath it, the Red Prince rode atop his crystal steed followed by the ranks of his marching soldiers.

"How—?" Jesse exclaimed. "W-what are they—?"

A roiling rumble of thunder answered him, followed by a blast of wind.

"They think that you have the light," the Princess replied.

"But how? What about Maggie? What about—?"

"You mean, did they find her?" the Princess quietly asked. "We don't know."

Watching the Red Prince herd his Soldiers like cattle, Jesse felt terribly alone.

A piercing pulse of light shot out from the Red Prince.

Instantly, the three Ambers started to vibrate.

"No!" Jesse pleaded with them, "Please! Don't leave! What do we do?" he cried. "Where do we go?"

"There!" the Princess urged, pointing to the distant mesas.

The Red Prince's grotesque face was twisted in greedy anticipation.

Baring his glittering red teeth, he pointed his blazing sword at the distant glow of the Ambers and laughed as they struggled to fly from his light.

"We haf nothing but time," he gloated.

"TIME!" his Soldiers roared, and they stamped in unison as the orange dust swirled about the shifting ground cracking beneath their feet.

"MARCH!" the Red Prince bellowed.

And they did.

The Ambers struggled to resist the pulsing light beckoning from the Red Prince's sword as the plume of orange dust grew larger and closer.

Helping the Princess over the fractured ground, Jesse realized that the fiery fissures spitting up magma and black smoke were not only increasing in number but getting wider.

The Princess stumbled.

Catching her, Jesse urged, "Come on! We can't stop!"

"Go! Go on, Jesse," she replied weakly. Her light was fading. "The mesas are too far . . . I'm too weak. I can't—"

"Yes, you can!" Jesse insisted. "You can't stop! You can't!"

The Ambers were no longer circling them but were drifting toward the Red Prince's approaching light. "Come here!" he commanded them. "Come here now! NOW!"

One Amber hesitantly obeyed; then the other two followed.

"Closer! Closer to my face!" Jesse demanded.

They glowed brighter, as did the Princess who shook her head and pleaded, "You need to go on without me, Jesse. The Red Prince—"

"No!" Jesse argued, helping her to her feet. Turning toward the distant mesas, he paused. Something wasn't right. Something didn't look right.

Jesse stared in disbelief.

A set of hills between them and the mesas was moving! Rising and falling like slow ocean swells, they were rolling beneath the cracked surface toward Jesse and the Princess.

"Stay close to us!" Jesse ordered the Ambers, and he pulled the Princess across a widening fissure, then another and another as he struggled to navigate the fracturing surface.

Surging into larger and larger swells, the crests of the approaching hills gave off snapping wisps and streaks of black smoke while seeming to roll even faster toward Jesse and the Princess.

A small swell rolled beneath them, and Jesse pulled Princess Amethyst to him as they struggled to keep their balance.

Chunks of the fractured earth were rising up out of the cracked crust. The chunks would sink between the rows of cresting waves and then rise higher, the widening cracks between them revealing a splashing sea of magma below.

The pieces pushed even higher, and Jesse watched in amazement as they became molten blobs with flaming holes for eyes and screeching mouths gushing fire.

Rising from the rolling sea of ignite, horrible faces poured forth lava and streaming tendrils of orange-and-white hair.

Burning heads were growing necks and shoulders!

Dripping with liquid fire, white-hot spears were thrust from the fiery depths by magma hands and arms swirling with white smoke.

They were Soldiers; rows upon rows of viscous white warriors roaring through liquid helmets and spewing fiery sprays of molten rock.

Beneath them, gaping horses' mouths gushed from the smelting surface. Streaming manes flew off reaching necks and trailed thin streaks of hot orange magma as the blazing white beasts galloped directly at Jesse and the Princess.

Searching frantically for a way out, Jesse thought he saw another set of rolling hills coming up behind the Red Prince's rear flank.

Pointing to the mesas where the horizon was still flat, Jesse grabbed the Princess.

"RUN!" he cried in panic.

"We can't!" she replied as she watched the nearest wave

of White Soldier/Horses race toward them. "We can't outrun them."

"We have to!" Jesse yelled.

Unable to endure the quickening pulse of the Red Prince's light, the three Ambers were darting erratically toward it.

"HOLD!" commanded the Princess and raised an open palm to the Ambers. Her entire body instantly darkened as light shot from the middle of her forehead and held them in an incandescent aura.

Immediately the glowing Ambers swooped back to Jesse and the Princess and began to encircle them in a streaking blur.

His stallion blindly stabbing at the shifting pieces of ground, the Red Prince saw Jesse and the Princess disappear in a cocoon of light before the charging army of molten white Soldier/Horses.

"FORWAARD . . . MOOVE FORWAARD!" the Red Prince screamed at his men, only to discover more waves of Soldier/Horses closing on his rear flank. But they weren't White Soldier/Horses . . . they were black!

Spinning in confusion, his Soldiers found themselves caught between colliding armies of white and black Soldier/Horses.

Roaring his rage, the Red Prince turned on his own Soldiers. "TO THAA LIIGHT! TO THAA LIIGHT!" he screamed over and over, and wheeling his blazing sword tips overhead, mercilessly cast violent pulses of light into their midst, driving them clawing over each other in the direction of the White Soldier/Horses.

Jesse and the Princess floated in a transparent eggshell of light.

The streaking Ambers emitted an ear-piercing whine, which kept climbing higher and thinner as it diced the rolling roar of the charging White Soldier/Horses into slivers of sound that exploded in staccato bursts and then disappeared into the silence of their cocoon.

His heart racing like the wing-beat of a frightened bird, Jesse stared up in horror at the gaping mouths of White Soldier/Horses screaming silently as the first looming wave soundlessly rose and came crashing onto him and the Princess.

Rupturing the cocoon of silence, the piercing roar and cry of battle blasted through the cocoon's spinning skin of light with the first White Soldier/Horses. Then their sound immediately evaporated into silence, and the fiery shapes slowed to an undulating dance of wavering spumes of lava lazily erupting into streaming arcs of fire.

The next wave tore through, and again its numbing howl instantly vanished.

Jesse couldn't move. He couldn't take his eyes off their melting faces and black eyeholes swimming in clouds of fiery smoke.

Not a foot away, a horse's black-and-orange eye slowly slid past.

Above it, a swirling plume of liquid fire became the seething edge of a jagged sword.

Jesse raised his hand to protect himself—and the brilliant blade ripped through him.

Crying out, he doubled over in pain, and the air felt cold at the back of his throat.

Suddenly it seemed that he was standing outside his body, watching the white-hot blade tear into him.

The rope of pain shrank to a searing wire of fire as the screams and cries repeatedly skewered his entire being.

He shuddered violently . . . then relaxed.

The paralyzing roar of war seemed farther off.

Someone called his name, but he couldn't tell from where.

He tried to take a breath, and as he did a sweet warmth filled him.

He imagined that the white-hot sword had penetrated his body, yet he wasn't hurt.

He looked to his wound, and realized that the raging Soldier/Horse had passed through him and he wasn't hurt!

Amazed, Jesse turned and beheld the Princess, ablaze with

light, standing over him, while wave after wave of Soldier/
Horses continued to gallop through them.

Echoing surges of violence permeated him as the
warriors twisted about, futilely slashing back at Jesse and the
incandescent Princess while being carried out of the cocoon in
a combust of confusion.

The pounding of Jesse's racing heart slowed.

His breath deepened. It filled his whole being, then released
into a warm rush of air that became a thousand voices that
grew into a deep reverberating "OHHHHHH" as the waves of
Soldier/Horses rode away like ghosts.

There was no cocoon of light to protect the Red Prince.

Slashing with rage from atop his faltering steed, he hacked
through endless surges of White Soldier/Horses.

Turning back to his battling men, he roared, "FIGHT!
FIGHT FOR THA LIGHT!" as the first Black Soldier/Horses
hit his rear flanks. Flashing with fury, he spun from White
army to Black, caught in the middle of their war.

"STAND YOUR GRROUND!" he raged. "STAAAND!"

The wave of Black Soldier/Horses collided with the front
line of White Soldier/Horses, and a great explosion of lava and
a booming clap of wind scattered the Red Prince's ranks and
nearly knocked him off his horse.

The inexorable swells and counter swells continued to carry the screaming Black and White Soldier/Horses into and through each other. They attacked one another regardless of color: black attacked black; white attacked black; black, white; and white, white. They fought and flailed, raising their flaming swords higher, even as their horses sank lower into the rolling magma, which relentlessly carried them out and away from each other like rippling rings from pebbles tossed onto water.

Through the cocoon's thinning light, Jesse could see the storming sea of lava subsiding as the screaming whine of the Ambers dropped to a crying hum.

The last threads of the cocoon's unraveling light had woven into a brilliant spiraling rope arching high above Jesse and the Princess.

Plunging back down toward a fiery whirlpool, it was grabbed by a massive hand that burst from the liquid fire. Wrapping the spinning cord of light in a balled fist, fingers like logs squeezed streams of lava from between boulder-sized knuckles.

A shivering point of light pierced the swirling surface and erupted into a monolithic sword of molten silver clenched in a second smoldering fist.

An immense trunk of an arm followed fist and sword. Then a huge pointed helmet, housing a head the size of a truck and spewing a plume of lava, rode upward atop the bulging neck, shoulders, and torso of a giant White Warrior.

Cascading chutes of lava poured off him as he rose upward, riding a fiery geyser that violently wrenched itself into a rearing white stallion.

A deafening roar erupted: "ALL HAIL IGNEUS THE NTH! ALL HAIL IGNEUS THE NTH!"

Towering high above Jesse and the Princess, the White Warrior's furious steed shed liquid silver, as the huge gladiator peered down at Jesse's tiny shape.

"I AM IGNEUS THE NTH! OF WHAT—OF WHERE—TO WHERE?" he rumbled thunderously.

Seeing the giant White Soldier/Horse tower over Jesse and the Princess a short distance away, the Red Prince screamed his rage as he viciously hacked through his battling Soldiers.

Suddenly a jarring tug on his two-bladed sword nearly lifted him from his saddle.

Streaming from both ends of the Prince's sword, twisting ribbons of light wove into a single black rope, which was grasped by the giant molten hand of a Black Warrior, who kept rising higher and higher till he loomed over the Red Prince.

Identical to the White Warrior in every way but color, the Black Warrior sat astride his rearing giant black steed, pointed his dripping molten sword at the amazed Red Prince, and roared, "I AM IGNEUS THE NTH! OF WHAT—OF WHERE—TO WHERE?"

"We are not Ignite!" Jesse yelled up at the White Igneus, who thrust the curved point of his burning blade to within inches of the Princess's face.

"OF WHERE? TO WHERE?" the great warrior roared again, swatting at the swarming Ambers. "YOU ARE BLACK?" he challenged.

"I am human," yelled Jesse, and indicated the darkening Princess, whose light was being sucked from her by the White Igneus's sword point. "And she is Princess Amethyst!"

"WE ARE WHIITE!" the White Igneus thundered, sitting tall and swelling his mountainous chest. Sweeping his enormous sword in a great circle above his Soldiers, he declared, "WE FIGHT FOR WHIITE!"

He pointed to the black Soldiers fighting his white Soldiers across the battlefield and roared defiantly, "THEY ARE BLACK! THEY FIGHT FOR BLACK!"

The identical Black Igneus was simultaneously pointing at the White Igneus and thundering, "THEY ARE WHIITE! THEY FIGHT FOR WHIITE!"

The circles upon circles of colliding Black and White Soldier/Horses were rolling farther and farther away as they sank deeper into the hot magma.

Jesse could see the Red Prince getting closer, slashing through the chaos of Soldiers. Shouting up to the great White Igneus, Jesse cried, "We are looking for—"

"OF WHERE? TO WHERE?" the White Igneus roared impatiently.

". . . TO WHERE?" echoed the voice of the Black Igneus.

"We are looking for Metamorphia!" Jesse screamed. "WHERE IS METAMORPHIA?"

Whirling about on their huge beasts, both Black and White Igneii roared with laughter and bellowed as one, "META . . . MORPHIA? META . . . MORPHIA? METAMORPHIA *IS*!" the swirling wind taking their voices away and then returning them echoing, "AND . . . IS . . . NOT! ALWAYS, AND . . . FOREVER!"

Rearing on their raging steeds, each saluted his respective army and declared, "WE HAVE FOUGHT VALIANTLY AND DIED WELL!"

The circles of Black and White Soldier/Horses continued

to collide with great purpose as both sides roared their simultaneous response, "HAVE . . . VANQUISHED . . . THE . . . FOE! . . . WILL . . . BE . . . REMEMBERED . . . FOR . . . OUR . . . GLORIOUS . . . COURAGE . . . AND . . . DETERMINATION!"

The remaining Soldier/Horses raised their fiery swords and charged each other yet again, roaring, "ALL HAIL!" even though some sank below the surface before ever reaching their enemy.

Garbled voices sang, "GAVE . . . TRUTH . . . TO . . . THE . . . NIGHT . . . THAT . . . . OUR . . . FLAG . . . WAS . . . STIILL . . . THERE!" as the nearly submerged Black and White Soldier/Horses crashed head-on, creating one great shoulder-to-shoulder circle that surged up and charged away from the fray as one.

His face twisting in anticipation, the Red Prince trampled the last of the Soldier/Horses and charged at Jesse and the Princess.

Jesse grabbed for the Princess's hand and desperately sought an escape.

Eyes bursting with red light, the Red Prince drove his crystal spurs into his mount's sides, and Jesse knew that he and the Princess were lost. There was no way out, no cocoon to protect them.

The Red Prince closed the remaining distance and lunged at Jesse, but to his amazement, the Prince's horse slowed to a stop while its legs still churned at a gallop.

Staring in confusion as the slicing point of his sword came to a halt inches from Jesse's chest, the Red Prince watched helplessly as the surging swell of Black and White Soldier/Horses lifted him and his mount.

Lashing at his confused horse, the Red Prince fought the rolling ridge, but it was too powerful and as he raged his astonishment, it carried him backward, away from Jesse and the Princess.

Smothering fingers of fiery magma reached off the wave's crest and encircled the arms and neck of the Red Prince and pulled him and his screaming Soldiers down into the boiling depths.

They were no more.

"He's gone!" Jesse whispered.

The Princess stared out at the small ripples in the vast, cracking crust that was all that remained of the Red Prince.

"He's gone," the Princess quietly concurred, her mind elsewhere.

Jesse saw the absent expression on her face. "He was your brother," he remembered.

The Princess nodded. "Yes. He was."

"How could he . . ."

". . . have been my brother?" The Princess asked.

Jesse nodded.

"We each have our own journey that we take, Jesse. Even brothers and sisters." She looked at him and smiled sadly. "They are a part of us, but they aren't us. No matter how much we try to make it otherwise."

I could feel Jesse thinking about how different he and I were, and how much we argued and fought.

"So, you loved him?" Jesse asked in disbelief.

The Princess nodded. "Once . . . upon a time," she whispered sadly.

Angry clouds rumbled in the distance.

Jesse helped the struggling Princess toward the nearest mesa. The weakly pulsing Ambers floated close by.

"Who won?" Jesse complained. "Nobody won! And how

can Metamorphia be 'always and forever' and 'be and not be'? That's a riddle! A stupid riddle!"

"Perhaps Metamorphia isn't a place," the Princess wondered aloud. "Perhaps it's a state of being—a state of being that is always becoming."

"How can something be 'always becoming'?" demanded Jesse, helping the Princess over a fiery split.

The Princess shrugged. "Because everything is always changing?" she suggested.

Jesse snorted. "You mean like 'morphing' is a part of 'Meta-*morph*-ia'—and everything is always morphing?"

The Princess nodded weakly.

Jesse stopped, his eyes widening fearfully. "Does that mean there is no such place as Metamorphia—and no such person as Metamorphos, the Wizard of Iz?"

Watching him, the Princess asked softly, "Is that what you believe?"

Jesse didn't know what he believed anymore. "If there is no Wizard of Iz, then how are we supposed to find the source of light?"

"There has to be a source of light, don't you think?" the Princess replied. "If there's a source, there ought to be some way to find it."

"So maybe there is a Metamorphia and a Wizard of Iz!" Jesse whispered hopefully.

Wishing she could be of more help, the Princess gently prodded him. "You can't know if you don't look."

"But where?" cried Jesse, impatiently.

"Everywhere; inside and out," answered the Princess.

"I can't . . ."

"Yes you can, Jesse. You have that choice."

"But what if I don't find it?" Jesse asked angrily.

"When you are looking, you are finding it."

"That doesn't make any sense."

"It will, Jesse."

"No it won't," Jesse insisted. "It won't make sense just because you say so!"

I knew he felt as if he were arguing with Mom.

The Princess couldn't say anything more. She was too tired.

Jesse turned in frustration toward the nearest mesa. "Fine!" he harrumphed and angrily pointed at the mesa. "We can start there!" Then he pointed at another and another. "And there, and there, and there," he said as he took the Princess's fading arm, and they started out.

THE DYING OF THE LIGHT

Jesse once brought me the chewed-up head of his ratty old teddy bear in one hand, the body in his other.

"Fix it!" he demanded, holding the pieces up to me.

I told him I couldn't.

"But it's broke!" he insisted. "Make like it's a boo-boo," he suggested with tears in his eyes.

"I'm not kissing that smelly old thing," I informed him.

He looked at me in confusion. "Don't you want to?"

"I can't fix it!" I yelled at him.

I don't know which I hated more: him making me feel so helpless, or myself for not being able to do anything about it.

What was Jesse doing? I could see that they were lost on

the magma plains, looking for something that wasn't there. If I could see him, why couldn't he see me? Why couldn't he hear my thoughts? I couldn't stop him, and he couldn't come back. We were running out of time.

"Stay there, Jesse," I whispered with my eyes shut. "Don't go any farther. Please . . ."

My heart sank as another ragged roar from the crowded Cathedral Square below crashed over the castle walls.

We had been taken back to the Royal Court. I stood with the others beneath the darkening walls of the great room as the dim and dismal Lords and Ladies listened nervously to Gneiss telling the "journey of the flashlight."

King Bloo sat sparkless and dull next to the very unhappy and ill-looking Green Queen. Faded to a dingy green, she perched expectantly and tried to follow Gneiss's rambling in spite of Pyrite's tarnished cubes clicketing at her feet. She smacked her fool, knocking off his other ear.

Still with a bit of glow, the twitching Orange Prince stood protectively beside Scheelite, who was trying to ignore the hideous olive-brown Lady Hiddenite hovering at the Prince's other shoulder, staring rocks at her.

Doing her best to look colorful, Torri stayed close to

Gneiss, while Pyrope and I listened near the tall crystal arches overlooking the Square.

I could barely see the outlying areas, as the rest of the kingdom had faded to a dingy gray punctuated by an occasional sputter of warm light.

Far below the opening, two crusty yellow peasants with little illumination between them were hurrying past the fallen figure of an old man lying beneath a darkening streetlamp. His crystal-and-garnet body seemed to be covered in a hoary yellow film that gave off small puffs of dust as he reached after the peasants, who disappeared into the crowded square in front of the Cathedral of Light.

What was once a brilliantly white shrine now cast a yellow pall over thousands of darkening and dull Chrystallians who were angrily chanting, "GIVE US LIGHT! GIVE US LIGHT!"

Twice ringing the Cathedral's walls, hundreds of Basalt Guards struggled to keep the crowd back as the Holy Clear appeared on a distant balcony and held up his faded arms to another soaring roar.

"BEHOLDA THA TOOA ANDA FROA!" he blessed the crowd. "BE WITHA THA TOOA AND FROA. YOU ARRA THA TOOA AND FROA—"

"'FRO' THIS!" someone yelled.

A tattered crystal girl of faded green and dirty tourmaline led a group of dim and chipped women who were yelling, "AH AM WOMAN! AH AM WOMAN!"

Linking arms, a muscular and dull gang of green granite men started chanting, "NO DARK! NO DARK!"

His diamonds pulsing dimly, the Holy Clear drew some irregular shapes in the air and then disappeared inside the Cathedral.

The crowd brayed its disapproval.

I turned back, and Gneiss was jabbing his chubby thumb at me.

"She was turnin' colors," he was explaining nervously, "an' dis Ambuh Girl, dis huge piece of Ambuh wid da very old girl-Human inside starts goin' to and fro wid da light of da Maggie Human an' gettin' lightuh and brightuh—really bright, and, uh . . ."

He stopped, his mica mouth hanging open as the Holy Clear appeared behind him beneath a crystal arch.

Inserting herself between the Orange Prince and Scheelite, Lady Hiddenite whined through her long olive nose, "This is hardly possible! Everybody knows Amber is impure. How can you believe that—?"

"How could something impure have light?" Princess Topaz interrupted, her voice cracking and her brilliant blue faded nearly to pasty white.

The crystal Court waited anxiously for Gneiss's answer.

"Well, see," he continued hesitantly, "da Amber Girl has dis, uh, 'DNA' stuff, right? It's like 'information,' about bein' alive, or havin' light." His splotches of mica flickered nervously as he waited for some sign of understanding.

All he got was silence.

"An' da Maggie Human," he rushed on, jabbing a rock thumb at me, "she has da same DNA stuff. It comes from where dey come from, da Humans"—he pointed down at the dull scuffed and scratched blue floor beneath us—"down," then he pointed up, "or up, or down . . . dere," he concluded, completely confused.

There was an uncomfortable clunking of crystal, and somebody coughed.

"Anyway," he kept on, "dese two are really glowin' and—"

"Glowing?" sneered the Holy Clear.

"Glowin'," Gneiss concurred with a vigorous nod. "Very definitely glowin', ya Holy Holiness . . ."

King Bloo abruptly sat up. "Za Princess! Vhere iss za Princess?" he demanded anxiously.

The Queen shifted uncomfortably on her dark throne as Pyrite dutifully straightened up and declared in a hoarse lisp, "Bloo-thee-Troo c-callth for thee Preentheth Ametheetht—"

Swatting him silent, the Queen knocked off his nose.

"And where isss Red-Prince-The-Next?" she hissed ominously, silencing the King with a look.

Sighing, the Orange Prince answered petulantly, "I haf alreddy told yoo. He ees on a meeshun! Zee meeshun to find zee light, oui? Zee flashlight?"

"ENOUGHA!" the Holy Clear commanded. "You say thatta their issa heaven? Thatta they arra gods?" he asked incredulously. "And thatta tha son offa godda has broughta tha lighta? You worship falsa idols! You arra blasphameengah!"

"Yah! Ziss is troo!" King Bloo instantly agreed, happy to have a ruling. "Ziss iss against za roolls! Za Human cannott 'become' za light!" he declared emphatically.

Wagging what was left of his head, Pyrite waved his one good arm up and down. "Up eeth up, an' down eeth down—exthept when up eeth down, an' down eeth—"

The Queen jerked his leash and he spit out another crystal tooth.

Seething, she turned to the Orange Prince. "Where iss my sson?" she demanded.

The Orange Prince's chin jumped sideways. "Oui. Zee Red Prince," he quickly replied, miffed that his own exploits weren't being appreciated, "he ees in zee Land of Magma, I seenk—by now—would be my guess."

"Your guesss?" the Queen sizzled, a dull mustardy flash rolling through her.

"Undt vere is za Princess Amessyst!" insisted King Bloo, remembering that he had not gotten an answer.

Smiling confidently, the Orange Prince adjusted his neck. He knew the answer to that question. "Our seester, Princess d'Ametheest—an' zee Jesse Huooman—haf dissappeared een zee great crushiing," he informed them.

The Royal Court gasped in surprise, and the King's mouth opened but nothing came out. The Orange Prince held up his hand reassuringly.

"Mais—but—zee Red Prince is pursueeeng zee light, zees is why he ordered me back to Beryl. An' eizer way we beleeff zee Huooman will return for hees seester!" he claimed, though still not absolutely clear on this strategy. "He will breeng zee light!" he announced victoriously. "Ziss is why I, 'Next to Zee Next'—"

"WHO HAS THE LIGHT?" someone shouted. "WHERE'S THE LIGHT!"

The Queen's leash hand shot straight up, nearly decapitating Pyrite.

"SSSILENCE!" she commanded.

Turning to her orange son, she hissed, "What if he doessn't find the Jessse Human? What if he doesn't bring back sssa light?"

"Yah!" the King mumbled dejectedly, still stunned with concern for his daughter. "Vhat if za Red doesn't bring back za light, hmmm? Haf you rooled out zat possibilitee, Orange? Undt za Princess? Vat about—"

The Royal Court erupted all over again, and the Orange Prince instantly broke out in a rash of angry yellow hives.

"S'il vous plaît! S'il vous plaît!" he cried. "I assure yoo, wee haf zis under control!" he promised, with a swallow and a twitch. "I haf every r-reason to belief—"

"You beleeeve?" the Queen incredulously inquired.

Slamming his ruler on the floor, the King angrily proclaimed, "HE BELEEFS!" then caught the Queen's ugly glare and quickly added, "I . . . guess."

"I have the light," I announced.

"Believing isss not knowing!" the Queen screamed at her husband.

An embarrassed hush fell over the Court.

"B-but za Princess Amethyst . . ." King Bloo demanded. "Vhat has happened to za Princess?"

"I HAVE THE LIGHT," I repeated, louder.

A voice called out, "What'd she say?"

"Who has the light?" another cried.

Gneiss grabbed me. "Not yet!" he whispered urgently.

Teetering on the edge of her throne, the Queen fixed her cat eyes on me "What did you sssaay?" she asked menacingly.

"I said, 'I have the light,'" I repeated for the third time, fear creeping into my voice.

His eyebrows jumping, the Orange Prince snorted. "Hah! Ziss is imposseeble!" he stated smugly. "Ziss is not posseeble."

I took the flashlight from my pocket.

Leaping to her feet, the Queen crushed Pyrite's leg.

"Yoo dooo!" the Orange Prince blurted. "How did yoo—? When did yoo—?"

The Holy Clear launched himself toward me, as did the Green Queen, yanking Pyrite after her and breaking off his other arm.

Lords and Ladies screamed excitedly, "SHE HAS THE LIGHT! SHE HAS THE LIGHT!"

Standing to get a better view, King Bloo demanded, "SILENCE! I vill haf silence! Zat is za rool!"

Gneiss was bowing quickly to the Holy Clear. "Ya Clear, if I may have a few woids," he requested urgently. "Da Jesse Human—like a dummy—insisted on tryin' ta find da Wizard of Iz and da source a' light," he smirked, holding out his hands and shrugging. "How? Right? He's Human! Not a chance!" he crowed. "Dat's why I brought back da flishlight."

All of a sudden this was about him?

Pretending humility, he quickly added. "It took a lotta work, but I didn' give up!"

I wanted to strangle him.

The Holy Clear stared at Gneiss in amazement. "He wenta to finda Metamorphos?" he gasped.

Gneiss nodded. "Yeah, dat's what I said—in Metamorphia, wid da Princess. Go figure."

"M-metamorrphoss?" stuttered the Orange Prince. "P-pourquoi—why?"

"Ta find da source a' da light," Gneiss blurted impatiently, then backpedaled immediately, "Dose were his words, not mine!"

"VAIT!" hollered the King, confused. "Who goes to Metamorphia?"

"An' den dere was a great crushin'!" Gneiss spluttered anxiously. "I mean, it wasn't da Fossilia crushin', not da way da Holy Clear described it." Catching himself, he turned to the Holy Clear in an effort to clarify. "I mean it was, but it wasn't. See, Fossilia is more about da sanwiches. Ya know, da layers of, uh—"

Reaching past Gneiss to take the flashlight from me, the Holy Clear was abruptly pushed aside by the Queen, who tried to grab it as well.

"No!" I cried, backing away.

The Holy Clear turned on the Queen and proclaimed, "It isa mya dootee!"

"It isss my right!" she shot back.

"It's my flashlight!" I yelled.

"Dat's what I wanted ta talk ta ya about," Gneiss quickly whispered to the Holy Clear, who was drifting up to me. He laid a crooked diamond finger on my wrist, as if he were taking my pulse, then quickly snatched Jesse's flashlight out of my hand.

Pointing it at the Queen, he declared. "I want thissa flasha-lightta for tha people! Not just forra thissa Houssa offa Clarritee."

Not about to give him the last word, the Queen proclaimed, "I—we are the POWER!" she claimed. "It isss ordained!"

A dim wave of light crackled across the facets of the Holy Clear's diamonds. "Youra subjects' belief issa youra power," he instructed the Queen. "Their beleif issa how you arra ordained!"

"Yesss!" challenged the Queen. "And your power?"

You could have heard a crystal click.

Bowing humbly to the Queen, the Holy Clear held the flashlight close to his chest and indicated the world outside.

"I-ah hafa no power. I, I ama tha humble servant anda messenger offa Metamorphos," he replied solemnly.

You could tell she knew that he had tricked her.

Pointing at me, he announced, "Tha Maggie Huooman willa presenta tha lighta to tha people offa Chrystallia!" Then he raised Jesse's flashlight for the whole Court to see. "So alla may bennefitta. So alla may know tha trootha! And tha lighta!" he proclaimed in his scratchy voice then gave the apoplectic Queen a small smile.

There were a lot of "Metabless-yous" and "Amens" as the Holy Clear turned his back on the Court and began to examine Jesse's flashlight.

Grabbing my arm, Gneiss whispered excitedly, "Look! Look at 'im! He don' know how ta turn it on. He don' know how ta turn on da flishlight!"

The Truth

Truth is something that is still there no matter how hard you try to avoid it.

I could see a fiery chasm separating Jesse and the Princess from the great black mesas.

I could see its towering black walls that seemed to float on the shifting ground.

With a deep groan, the magma-splashing mouth between them and the mesa opened wider. A wind stirred as the Dragonfly, Butterfly, and Wasp Ambers circled above them.

"Jesse . . ." Princess Amethyst whispered, barely able to speak.

"We can jump!" Jesse insisted. "When the chasm gets smaller again, we can jump."

The Princess's light dimmed even more. "I can't, Jesse," she tried to explain. "I haven't got—"

"NO! We'll give you more light!" Jesse cried, and he ordered the Ambers, "Come here! Come closer!"

"Jesse," the Princess persisted, "you need their light. The Ambers are here for you. This is your journey. Yours alone."

"But I don't want to go alone!" Jesse pleaded.

There was a deep snap, and the ground beneath them shook as the wind gusted.

"Don't leave me!" he cried.

Reaching out with her darkening hand, she touched his cheek. "I have to, Jesse. It's time."

"But what if—?"

"What *is*," interrupted the Princess. "Think of what is—not what if," she directed him. "And try to remember that you can choose, Jesse. Right now . . . you can choose. Believe that you can choose—now, when you are scared. Especially when you are scared."

"I don't understand!" Jesse cried.

"Jesse," urged the Princess, "remember the Amber Girl's words: 'Your fears are like dragons, guarding your greatest treasures.'"

Jesse didn't want to remember any words. "No! I don't—I can't!" he whined as the groaning chasm grew smaller and the wind swirled.

"Yes, you do, Jesse," she insisted. "You remember; that

which scares you most can wake you to your greatest power," she explained softly. "Go!" she urged him. "Go, Jesse—and know that I will be with you."

A flurry of cracks ripped through the ground, and the chasm began to widen again.

"Go, Jesse. Now—while you can!" the Princess entreated as the wind began to howl.

Jesse turned to the Amber Wasp and Butterfly. "Stay here," he commanded. "Stay with her!"

"Come," the Princess whispered, and they did. The Dragonfly Amber came closer to Jesse and started to pulse brightly.

Jesse couldn't let go of the Princess's hand. "I'll never forget you," he promised.

"Nor I, you," she whispered.

There was a loud CRAACK, and the fiery mouth widened.

"Go, Jesse!" Princess Amethyst urged.

Jesse couldn't. "It's too wide," he cried, shrinking from the spitting magma.

With a deep groan, the chasm opened further.

"Now!" she commanded him.

Jesse hesitated—then ran as fast as he could and leapt. His arms desperately flailed and his legs ran at the air . . . and he knew immediately that he wasn't going to make it to the other side.

Then the white light of the Dragonfly Amber was just inches from his face, and Jesse's hand was slowly, desperately reaching for it.

It jumped out of reach, and Jesse's mouth opened wide as he strained to reach for it again . . . and again . . .

Suddenly his foot banged into the far edge of the chasm then slipped off the edge as his chest slammed into the rock wall, his breath bursting from him with a painful cry.

He was sliding backward into the burning magma.

Tearing at the ground, he tried to grab on to something, anything . . . two of his fingers found the smallest of cracks . . . then ripped loose.

He was falling again!

Crying out in pain, he fought to hold on to the crumbling earth.

His tearing fingernails found another crack, and he knew that he had but one chance.

With a cry he painfully pulled himself up over the edge and rolled onto his back, gasping for breath.

The Princess!

Frantically scrambling to his feet, he yelled her name.

There was no sign of her.

He felt lost and hopeless. How was he going to find Metamorphos! How was he ever going to get home? He wanted to sit down and cry.

The Dragonfly Amber floated uncomfortably close to his eye and he swatted it away. It came back, and he swatted it away again. It circled him once . . . then flew off into the dark mouth of a canyon.

Jesse had no place else to go. So he followed.

The roar of the angry crowd brought me back as an angry red-and-purple ripple of light washed through the walls of the cavernous Cathedral.

Surrounding us, a circle of Basalt Guards stood at attention, their lifeless mica barely reflecting the failing light.

Within the towering interior, great blue crystal pillars soared to the ceiling, their razor-sharp edges knifing upward alongside thousands of straight and shattered lines of dull light that crisscrossed endlessly beneath their transparent surfaces.

Jutting out at odd angles from the tops of the crystal columns, huge multicolored mineral formations supported a darkening crystal dome.

Veins of gold and silver ran like lightning through the vast walls. Twisting and threading 'round and through each other, they wove into great glinting ropes that collected at the front of the Cathedral into a bejeweled altar made of three great knots. Suspended high above the altar by a single silver cord, a massive diamond dimly pulsed with light.

Fussing with her fading colors, Torri stood alone as Gneiss yapped at the Captain of the Guards, who was staring straight ahead and didn't seem all that interested in what Gneiss had to say.

Pyrope and Scheelite held hands and stared into the vast crystal spaces.

"This must be beautiful when it is filled with light!" she whispered, trying to stay positive.

Pyrope could only nod.

"This is a good thing, isn't it?" she asked uncertainly. "Everybody will get light. There'll be no more fear. We'll be sent back to Sedentia—"

"I'll be sent back," Pyrope interrupted. "You'll stay here."

"You don't know that," argued Scheelite. "We don't know that."

Pyrope shook his head. "The Orange Prince will see to it," he stated soberly.

"I won't let—"

"Yes, you will," Pyrope insisted. "We don't have a choice. You know that."

Refusing to accept the finality of it all, Scheelite grasped at hope. "I'll talk to him. I'll tell him I have to go with you—that I don't belong here. I belong with you in Sedentia. We can't be split up."

"We've already been split up," Pyrope replied bitterly.

"I'd rather be without light!" she cried, though she knew he was right.

There was no way to know what they'd do with us after the Holy Clear turned on the flashlight. I had been wrong to listen to Gneiss, and I hated myself for it.

A loud roar shimmered jaggedly through the walls as Gneiss limped over to us, a big smile cracking his granite puss.

"Okay, okay, lissen up—lissen up! Dis is what's gonna happen," he announced to all of us. "Da Captain a' da Guards is gonna bring back da Holy Clear, or da Captain will come back an' take me an' Maggie to da Holy Clear, 'cuz—and get dis—da Holy Clear duzzn't know how ta work da flishlight!"

"How do you know that?" asked Scheelite.

"Well, Maggie can wuhk it!" chimed Torri.

Gneiss nodded his head. "Exactly!" he replied confidently. "Maggie knows how. So da Holy Clear needs Maggie, and 'cuz he needs Maggie, he'll hafta listen!"

"Listen to what?" I asked, confused.

Turning away from the others, Gneiss mumbled, "Ya know, like we discussed—goin' ta da Land of Air. Don' worry, dis is gonna be—"

"How do you know he can't make the light?" Scheelite asked again.

Sighing irritably, Gneiss explained, "'Cuz he already woulda if he coulda!" Filled with his own brilliance, he demanded, "Didn' ya see how he examined da flishlight when he took it from Maggie? He didn' know which end was which!"

"Excuse me," interrupted Pyrope, "but what exactly did you discuss with Maggie?"

Gneiss shook his head. "It's not important. Da point is we still have da flishlight and—"

"No, we don't," I reminded him. "The Holy Clear has it."

"I didn' promise anyone anythin'!" Gneiss replied defensively. "We discussed probabilities," he sputtered, and nervously nodded to me for confirmation, "and da likelihood dat da Holy Clear knows more den he lets on and dat maybe, maybe it was possible he could help her go back ta, you know . . . da Land of Air—"

"And you told Maggie that there was no Wizard of Iz, didn't you?" Pyrope asked. "Because you don't believe, and Maggie's too scared to believe. Is that why you stole the flashlight, so she and you wouldn't have to go to the Land of Magma?"

"Hey! I didn' steal nothin'," Gneiss squawked in objection. "I wuz thinkin' a' what wuz best for everybody."

I knew Pyrope was right.

"You weren't thinking of everybody, Mr. Gneiss," I said reproachfully.

He started to protest, but I wouldn't let him. "You were thinking only of yourself," I pointed out, furious with myself. "I know that, because you and I 'think like cousins.' Isn't that what you said—because we're so alike? Because that's all *I* was thinking of—me!"

Shrugging, Gneiss whined, "What difference does it make? We're all still gonna get light."

"Not all," Scheelite replied quietly. "Not Baz."

Not Baz; never again Baz.

The crowd's roar flashed like dull lightning in the Cathedral's walls.

"Or Jesse," I whispered. "I may never see my brother again. I may never see my mother or father, or Molly and Blue, because we don't know what the Holy Clear is going to do after they get the light."

The mob's roar pierced my heart.

I wanted to cry.

I took Scheelite's hand. "They want the light to take away their fear. So do I," I confessed, filled with remorse. "The truth is I've hated you because you were always so afraid—and because you reminded me that I was so afraid."

Shaking her head, Torri gushed breathlessly, "We ah about tuh get some moah laaght!" she exclaimed. "Ah miss Baz as much as anybuhdy, an' Jesse too, but we ah heah, and we ah all goin' tuh be beeootihful!"

"But we're not going to *feel* beautiful, Torri," I replied. "I always wanted to be beautiful like my friends——like you—— because I was afraid I was nothing if I wasn't beautiful. But I never felt beautiful. No amount of flashlight is going to make us feel beautiful."

Gently putting her hand on my arm, Torri whispered, "You . . . ah . . . beauhtaful!"

Crystal drums began a deadly beat that pushed the dimly lit walls into a trembling pulse.

"Why are we talkin' like dis?" Gneiss complained impatiently. "Dis is nothin' but good news! We're gettin' light, we're givin' light——"

"Did you forget what Jesse said," Pyrope reminded everybody, "that this light comes from batteries and that it is only temporary——it is not forever and it will die? What will happen then? And what about the Amber Girl?" Pyrope continued. "When she and Maggie glowed? That was proof that there's another source of light!"

"We don' know dat," Gneiss insisted.

Pyrope's dull light surged as he obstinately shook his head.

"What I know is what I feel. The light from the Ambers was different!" he insisted.

He was right. The light from the Ambers was different, and I had been too afraid to admit it.

Desperately grasping at hope, Scheelite asked, "But doesn't that mean—?"

Gneiss rode right over her. "Nothin'! It means nothin'," he argued. "We got light—dey need light! Have a little faith! We got—"

The mob's roar drowned his words as the Cathedral doors swung open.

His diamonds sputtering weakly, the Holy Clear stood in a white phosphorus chariot that glowed dully before two columns of Basalt Guards. He clutched Jesse's flashlight in one hand and gestured to me with the other.

Thinking that he was the one the Holy Clear wanted to see, Gneiss started forward, only to be stopped by a Basalt Guard.

Two other Guards appeared at my side.

"Wait!" I cried.

I reached for Pyrope's crystal hands. "I don't know what's going to happen. . ." A knot was growing in my chest. "But I need to say something to you because, right now, you are the closest thing I have to Jesse—I mean, you *are* Jesse; I know that now—and I need to tell you . . . to tell Jesse, to tell my little brother, that I . . . I . . ." I couldn't continue. All I wanted was to hold my brother's hand once more.

The crowd's roar washed over us.

Separating me from Pyrope, the two Guards pinioned my arms and marched me over to the Holy Clear, who clung to the side of the dim chariot like a bird of prey.

"LIGHT—LIGHT—LIGHT!" the hoary crystal crowd chanted, pushing at the expressionless Basalt Guards as we waded into the packed square.

Waving the flashlight and all it promised above the raised chipped and murky faces, the Holy Clear appeared solemn and stern as the portent of light made even the dimmest and sickest cheer.

The good mood infected Torri. She actually waved to me as she strolled alongside Pyrope and Scheelite, who were smiling bravely and following Gneiss as he sauntered ahead of them, beaming and waving like a politician on parade.

Protected from the surging crowd by a thick collar of Basalt Guards, the entire House of Clarity packed the elevated Royal Crystal Boxes with an air of forced festivity.

King Bloo and the Green Queen, who wasn't green any longer, wore expectant smiles, trying to appear positive, even as the Queen's shaking hand grasped Pyrite's leash, which was still attached to his limbless pile of cubes.

The Orange Prince's failing light had turned the same olive brown as the horrid Lady Hiddenite, who leaned possessively on his arm. His light surged the moment he spied Scheelite, and he abruptly left the surprised Lady Hiddenite and descended importantly from the Royal Box.

Watching with dread as the foppish Prince approached ahead of his escort of Guards, Scheelite shrank from his silly grin.

Pyrope tried to protect her, but two of the Guards came forward and forcibly separated her from him, placing her on the Orange Prince's arm. The crowd cheered, and the Prince acknowledged them with a casual wave.

The procession came to a halt, and the drums stopped.

Waddling up to the chariot, Gneiss waved his hand at the Holy Clear, who stood stoically above him. "Psst! Ya Honor, Ya Grace, Holy a' Holies"—he fawned and leaned in confidentially—"just a quick woid. Look, da Maggie Human wants ta go home," he explained rapidly. "She doesn't wanna bother us. She's very sad, misses her friends, family, da air— misses her animals." He shrugged. "Go figure. Did I mention dat she'd leave da, er, flishlight?"

Ignoring him, the Holy Clear raised his arms to the crowd and waited for silence.

"We haava suffer-red tha Toa anna Froa!" he cried, lifting his ancient voice as the hoary horde hung on his every word.

"We hava lived inna lighta since beforra memorry, yet we tremble inna tha approacheeng darkanessa," he declared.

My heart was pounding in my ears.

"Nowa we question oura faitha," he continued gravely. "We aska tha 'whys': 'Whya hasa thissa happened?' 'Whya arra we here?' Anna we hava been told thata we 'becama' when tha Huoomans arriveda," he declaimed, pointing at me. "This issa what tha Maggie Huooman hasa told us!"

A great cheer soared and was followed by more chanting of "LIGHT! LIGHT! LIGHT!"

He let the clamor continue, then held his thin hands high.

The crowd immediately hushed.

"Anna I-ya," he cried, his ancient fist slowly beating on his dull chest, "I-ya, who standa humbled beforra you," he avowed, with small explosions of light sparking off his diamond body, "humbled beforra tha Greata Metamorphos, Wizard offa Iz! I-YA—I-ya, who only serve tha will offa tha people bya tha grace offa Metamorrrphos!" he cried, falling to his knees, "I-ya can only bowa beforra a higha power. I-ya canna only kneel beforra . . . THA CREEATORR OFFA LIIGHTA."

And he bowed to me!

"CREATOR OF LIGHT!" the crystal people cried, and pushed against each other to get even closer.

In the excitement, Pyrite's cubes started rearranging themselves until the Queen stepped on him and sizzled, "Oh, get on wiss it, for crissstal's sssakes!"

King Bloo kept asking, "Who undt how many are allowed? Vhat iss za rool?"

Raising Jesse's flashlight, the Holy Clear held it before me as the Royal Court of Beryl swooned in anticipation.

"You saya you canna give ussa your lightta," rasped the Holy Clear. "You saya you canna do this."

The crystal crowd hushed expectantly.

"SO—DO SO!" he commanded, thrusting the flashlight at me as a hungry roar went up.

My knees went weak.

Yelling to the Holy Clear over the noise, Gneiss insisted, "Dere's still an agreement dat gotta be made! She wants ta go home an'—"

"Shea wantsa toa go home?" the Holy Clear interrupted, regarding me from his knees. "You wanta toa go home?"

I opened my mouth to answer, but I could only nod.

"Bene. Good," he smiled benevolently then placed the flashlight in my hands. "Firsta tha lighta."

Hollering over the growing hysteria, Gneiss yelled in my ear, "I tink dis is da only choice!"

"But what about Jesse?" I cried.

Gneiss shrugged. There was obviously nothing he could do. There was nothing I could do, either.

Chanting "WE—WANT—LIGHT," the starving mass broke through the Guards' ranks and stopped only when the Holy Clear held up his hand for silence.

The deafening din subsided.

I knew it was time.

The only thing I could hear was my breathing and the clickety-click of thousands of crystals vibrating in anticipation.

I twisted the ring on the flashlight and slid it back.

A solitary soprano keened in the distance.

My hand shook as I pushed the button.

It was stuck.

Guessing it was because of all the dust and dirt, I blew on it.

The crowd oohed.

I banged the flashlight with my palm.

The crowd aahed.

I pushed the button again; it went in—but nothing happened.

I pushed it again . . . and again as an angry rumble rolled through the square.

Watching me with a blank stare, the Holy Clear gestured to two of the Basalt Guards to help him stand.

Desperately, I hit the flashlight against my leg and pushed the button again.

A beam of light shot out.

Ricocheting off the Cathedral, it split—then split again and again and again.

The Holy Clear jumped back in surprise, and the crystal people stared with eyes wide and mouths agape as the beams crashed through them.

Screaming and laughing, the Royal Court leapt to its feet, bathed in shooting shafts and singing splinters of light.

The Basalt Guards began vibrating so hard they couldn't hold their line.

The light went out.

The laughter died into cries of confusion.

Frantically I shook the flashlight.

The bulb flickered and glowed brighter—then died.

Banging on the flashlight, I kept repeating, "Let me try again! Let me try again!"

The throng waited in silence.

"It's the batteries!" I kept mumbling. "It's the batteries!"

The Holy Clear held out his hand. "Iffa you willa permit me?" he wheezed with a small smile.

Pyrope and Scheelite, Torri, and Gneiss stared at me, lost.

Cooing softly, the Holy Clear whispered, "You do notta haf alot offa choice nowa, do you, my child?" he asked, his smile freezing on his diamond face. "Anna neither do I-ya!" he added, his eyes wide with finality.

Slowly taking Jesse's flashlight from my hand, he held it up for everyone to see.

A ragged line of yellow-white light rippled up his diamond body.

"DO YOU FOR-RSAYKA YOUR CR-REATOR-R?" he shrieked at the stunned masses. "DO YOU BELIEVA SO EASIILY INNA SUCHA LIES?"

There was a scatter of cries as the Chrystallians shook their heads and murmured apologetically.

The darkened square dimmed even more, and the crowd gasped at the lessening light.

Pointing his dagger of a diamond finger at me, the Holy Clear glowered at his flock. "They brought thissa falsa light anna you for-rsook your Lorda Metamorphos!" he scolded.

Cries of anguish and fear answered him.

A pale-yellow-and-green Lady fainted, and a man of gray-and-black crystals collapsed on the ground, wailing his shame.

Ignoring them, the Holy Clear started to tremble. "They broughta you lies anna you abandonata your Cr-reator! They broughta you pr-romisses anna you wor-rshipped them assa gods!" he charged.

The crystal people began beating themselves about their heads and shoulders.

"You-a wor-rshipped their lighta assa tha tr-rootha!" he rebuked and paused, letting his words assault the miserable creatures.

"ANNA—IT—ISSA—NO—MOR-RA!" he declared. "Their lighta hassa DIED! It hassa died because itta issa notta tha tr-roo lighta! It hassa died because they arra FALSA GODS! They arra BLASSPHAMIATTAS!"

"BLASPHAMIATTAS!" the crystal people roared in reply, relieved to have anger take the place of their fear.

Falling again to his knees, the Holy Clear closed his eyes and reached his thin arms up to Metamorphos.

"I-ya pray forra your forgiveness, ourra Father, forra I-ya too believed!" he solemnly confessed, and started wagging his head back and forth.

"We musta alla begga forra forgiveness!" he ranted. "We musta offer ourra sorries, for we arra children—ANNA THA BLASPHAMIATTAS HAVA NO LIGHTA!"

The whole square erupted: "NO LIGHT! NO LIGHT!"

Pointing at me with hate in his eyes, he cried, "Theya hava only lies anna deceitta!"

"LIES AND DECEIT!" the Chrystallians thundered.

"They hava taken ourra lighta!" he rasped. "Poisoned ourra worlda! Defiled anna destr-royed ourra Mather, ANNA THEY—WILLA—BEA—CRRRRUSHED!"

Cries of "STONE THEM! CRUSH THEM!" reverberated until the ground shook.

Scheelite fainted at the Orange Prince's feet.

"No!" cried Torri, trying to stand.

Pyrope ran to Scheelite, desperately pleading to the screaming mob. "Listen! Listen to the truth!"

And Gneiss was dragged back to the others, saying over and over, "Dis is unfair, unconstitutional. Dis is unlawful. Dis is . . ."

THE SOURCE OF LIGHT

I don't understand death.

When Rocky, our dog died, Jesse was beside himself. He kept asking when Rocky would come back.

"He's never coming back," I insisted.

"Maybe he never left," Mom replied. "Though our bodies die, our true self lives on."

"Where?" asked Jesse. "Can I visit him?"

"Yes," Mom answered, "inside yourself. If you get really quiet and listen very carefully, to your thoughts and memories you can find him in your heart. He's always there."

"And when I die?" Jesse asked, unconvinced. "Where do my memories go?"

"They go wherever you've been, to whomever you've touched in your life," she replied.

"But they've never met Rocky," Jesse complained.

"They have . . ." Mom smiled, "in you."

The Dragonfly Amber chased after Jesse's shadow as it leapt along the jagged canyon walls.

I knew he had no idea where he was going. The canyon had split almost as soon as Jesse had entered it. It split again and again as the space between the walls kept getting narrower and their surface smoother, almost mirror-like.

There was a deep, wrenching groan, and Jesse wheeled about, listening. Voices? Were those voices?

In the light of the vibrating Ambers, it seemed as if hundreds of people were slowly moving past him in groups inside the deep reflection of the walls—clusters of people staring at him with frightened eyes and open mouths.

Grabbing the Dragonfly Amber, Jesse held it up and peered into the wall.

He tried to see who they were and realized that it wasn't the people who were moving; it was the wall—it was sliding sideways!

Stepping back, he cracked his head painfully on the wall behind him. It was closer than he had thought, and it was moving as well. The two walls were not only sliding in opposite directions—the space between them was shrinking. Horrified, Jesse realized that he was going to be crushed.

"Help! Somebody . . . help me!" he cried out.

The light dimmed and the voices grew louder. Jesse thought he heard them calling out to him, but he couldn't understand what they were saying.

Flattening his back against the deadly nudge of the groaning wall behind him, he reached for the pulsing Dragonfly Amber and held it up to the facing wall.

There was a familiar face. He couldn't quite place it; it was saying something to him, but he was unable to make out the words. Then another face took its place, and another.

The next one looked like our father!

"Dad?" Jesse whispered, amazed.

The face became Uncle Billy's.

"Uncle Billy?" Jesse cried, and then it became Cody's, then Aunt Doris's. "Stop! Wait!" Jesse cried through his own reflection in the smothering wall. "Who are you?"

"I . . . AM." many voices answered as the faces continued to morph into King Bloo, Pyrite, Princess Amethyst—

"Metamorphos?" yelled Jesse. "Are you Metamorphos?"

"E . . . V . . . E . . . R . . . Y . . . W . . . H . . . E . . . R . . . E . . . " the voices answered.

The wall inched closer.

"Where?" demanded Jesse.

"Every . . . where." they echoed.

"Are you the Wizard of Iz?" Jesse cried. "Please! Help me! Please!" He pressed his forehead against the unforgiving surface and started to sob.

"I'm scared!" he cried. "I'm so scared!"

A single soft voice, calm and clear, washed through him:

"'SCARED' . . . IS . . . NOT . . . *WHO* . . . YOU . . . ARE . . . JESSE."

It was our mother's voice!

Jesse looked up.

The morphing faces had become her face—our mother's face!

"Mom?" Jesse whispered.

"Scared is not who you are, Jesse," her voice repeated, though her lips didn't move.

"Please . . ." he begged. "I'm scared!"

"A *part* of you is scared, Jesse," her voice replied. It seemed to come from all around him.

Jesse shook his head. "Please!" he cried. "Please help—"

"Is there a part of you that isn't scared?" her voice asked. "Can you find that part of you that isn't scared?"

"No! I can't!" Jesse cried angrily as the walls shifted again with a dull moan. He collapsed on the ground and began to weep.

"Close your eyes, Jesse," her voice instructed.

Jesse couldn't understand. "Why?" he whined.

"Close your eyes," she whispered calmly.

Wrapping his arms about himself, he held on to himself, closed his eyes and began rocking back and forth.

"Can you *see* your fear, Jesse?" his mother's voice asked. "Can you see exactly *where* in your body you can feel your fear?"

"No! I can't!" he insisted petulantly. "I can't see anything!"

"Does the top of your head feel afraid?" her voice quietly asked. "Does the bottom of your foot, the back of your right hand—"

"No! No! Okay?" he shouted at her reflection.

"Look inside yourself, Jesse!" she commanded. "Look inside and find the part of you that isn't scared."

"I . . ."

"There is a place that isn't scared, Jesse," she quietly insisted. "Where is that place, Jesse? Find it!"

"Okay!" he replied impatiently, and then realized that he could. "Okay . . . yes, there's a place. But I . . ."

"Breathe, Jesse . . . breathe," she whispered. "If you can see that place where there is no fear—"

"Yes! Okay, I can see it . . ."

"Then can you see yourself sitting there?" she asked.

And Jesse realized that he actually could see himself sitting there, seated between the walls.

"Can you see yourself feeling the thundering of your heart?" she continued.

"Yes!" Jesse replied, amazed. "But why . . . ?"

"Can you see yourself listening?" Mom's voice whispered, "That place . . . that place from which you are seeing yourself, that place from which you are able to watch yourself feeling your fear, see yourself as you listen . . . and even think . . . that . . . is your place of *knowing*, Jesse."

Her voice rippled and vibrated through him.

"Your place of knowing—which is a part of *all knowing*. All knowing, of which everything that is, everything that exists is made; all knowing, to which you and everything belongs!"

Jesse felt a strange sensation, as if he were apart *from* everything around him—the walls, the voices—and yet he felt a part of everything at the same time.

He could feel the fear in his belly and the wall pushing on his back—and he could see himself as he was feeling these things!

"*You* are not your fear, Jesse, and your fear is not you."

His mother's voice flowed with the rush of his own breath.

"Your fear is your friend, Jesse . . .

"It is there to remind you of your *place of knowing* . . .

"You *are* the knowing, Jesse. You are the knowing that can *see* and watch yourself see.

"You are the knowing that can witness yourself feel . . .

"Your place of knowing, Jesse, your awareness . . . *is who you are.*"

His eyes were still closed, but Jesse could actually see himself— a tiny figure sitting between the closing walls with the Amber Dragonfly pulsing brightly in his hand.

"Your fears are like dragons, guarding your greatest treasure."

He saw himself atop the canyon, then high above the entire mesa.

"Your greatest treasure, Jesse, is your *knowing*, for it is the 'all' of which everything is: God, Love, Truth."

The walls groaned closer, and Jesse's mother's voice became his own.

"This is who you are, Jesse."

"This is what you belong to."

The black mesa walls shuddered . . . and then with a deep groan . . . slowly came together.

The light of the Amber Dragonfly wavered, blinked, and then disappeared into the wall with Jesse's hand . . . then his arm . . . and then his entire body.

FORGIVENESS

Jesse once broke my favorite doll, and I was so angry I said I wanted to kill him.

Mom said it was an accident and that I should forgive him.

"No!" I cried. "I can't ever forgive him."

"Can you forgive yourself?" Mom asked.

"For what?" I exclaimed in disbelief. "I didn't break it!"

She nodded her head.

"Can you forgive yourself for not being able to do anything to change that?"

I couldn't understand it. Jesse was gone.

My brother was no more . . . but my heart felt light . . . so light that I couldn't feel my body. Everything about me was a blur.

Faint sound washed from a silent horizon . . . then suddenly erupted into a deafening wall of screams crashing over the dusty, dim helmets of the Guards that encircled us.

"Let her speak . . . Let her speak!" Pyrope pleaded across the line of Guards to the crazed crowd.

A Guard brutally knocked him to the ground, and my stomach froze.

He tried to stand back up, but he couldn't, and he sat dazed and stunned, looking as if he didn't know where he was.

Shaking uncontrollably, Scheelite went to him and took him into her arms.

Torri stood, faded but tall, fighting not to flinch at each angry roar.

"Torri!" I called.

She gave me a sad smile. "It's okay tuh end an' nevuh be beautihful. It's okay!" she whispered as if to herself.

"But you are beautiful," I assured her. "You are very beautiful!"

Her crystal hand fluttered to her face. "Am ah?" she asked like a child. "Am ah really beautihful?"

"Now more than ever," I said. "Inside and out."

"We ah all beautihful—ahn't we?" she exclaimed, her eyes shining.

I nodded and forced a smile, even though I wanted to cry. The Guards began pushing the crystal people back.

"Now what are dey doin'?" demanded Gneiss.

"They're making room." I answered numbly, unable to stop thinking that this was all going to be over in a few moments. "Room for more people to hit us with those very large pieces of rock that they're tearing from the ground." It somehow felt better saying it out loud.

"Dis is all a big misunderstandin'! Isn't it?" Gneiss cried, turning to me in terror. "You have da light! You can make da light!"

"No, I can't."

"Of course ya can!" he argued frantically. "You make some light, and I'll find a way ta get us outta here. Trust me."

"There isn't any more light," I explained. "The batteries are dead."

"But dere's a way!" he panicked. "Dere's always a way! Can't ya—?"

"No, I can't," I interrupted, putting an end to it. I was tired of fighting.

A high stinging whine pierced the roar of the crowd.

Shooting straight up from the center of the darkening square, a brilliant blue beam of light sent the crystal creatures scrambling over each other in panic.

My heart leapt!

At the bottom of the blue column sat Jesse, his eyes closed, holding a brilliantly glowing Amber in his left hand.

"It's him! It's the other one!" a voice cried out. "It's the Jesse Human!"

"JESSE!" I screamed in relief, and the shaft of light instantly disappeared.

He was back! He was alive!

"DO NOTTA BELIEVA!" the Holy Clear cried out to the crowd. "He issa EVIL! He has notta thah troo lighta! He issa taking your-ra lighta!"

An ugly rumbling swelled from the seething mass.

"Tayka them!" the Holy Clear commanded. "Offer-r thema uppa to Metamor-rphos! Throw your selves onna Hissa mer-rcy! For only He-a canna save you!"

The Royal Court raised their hands to Metamorphos as the

Guards battled the crushing rush of crystal people and dragged Jesse over to us.

Bewildered, Jesse kept blinking as if he had just woken from a deep sleep.

"Jesse." I cried, holding onto him for dear life.

"I did it!" he muttered, dazed. "I moved!"

"The light is dying," I shouted over the crowd's roar. "They want to kill us. The flashlight—"

The already dim light of Chrystallia pulsed even darker as the crowd pushed to get at the light of the Amber Dragonfly.

The Holy Clear cried out, "They ARRA EVIL!" and the people screamed in fear.

Holding the glowing Amber Dragonfly high above his head, Jesse turned to them, and a hush immediately blanketed the square.

"We are not evil," he called out to them. "We are—"

The flashlight clattered to the ground at Jesse's feet, its lens shattering amid a chorus of surprised "Ohhhs!"

"Then give us tha lighta," the Holy Clear replied, "tha lighta thata you holda in youra hand!" Then pointing to his crystal flock he demanded angrily, "Give them their-ra lighta!"

The echo of his ancient voice hung like a shroud over the entire square.

The people of Chrystallia waited expectantly.

"This light comes from inside of me." Jesse tried to explain, "I don't know how . . . or why, but I know," he declared. "Just as it's inside all things . . . all of us. I cannot give you this light. It is not mine. I can only tell you—"

"What?" the Holy Clear interrupted in mock surprise and indicated the glowing Amber. "You hava notta tha lighta?"

"We are all light," Jesse tried to explain.

There was a rumble of confusion.

Spreading his long, thin fingers above Jesse's head, the Holy Clear pleaded to the multitude. "He say he issa lighta, yet he cannot give ussa tha lighta! He holds tha smalla Ambah, and takes tha naymma offa Metamor-rphos inna vain, yet he cannot give ussa tha lighta! He issa blasphamiatta! He issa falsa!"

An ugly roil of resentment rolled through the packed square.

"Metamorphia is not a place!" Jesse declared, and gasps and cries shot from the murky mass.

"Metamorphos is change," he insisted passionately. "It is not a person, or a god," he reasoned. "Metamorphia is 'being'! Being is change. It is the only thing that is eternal! It is the only thing that always is!" he exclaimed. "Change is . . . the Wizard of Iz!" he stated with great certainty.

Echoing into a jumble of words, his voice was swallowed by the silence of the crystal creatures as they stared at him with no understanding.

Weakly raising his trembling arms, the Holy Clear closed his still brilliant eyes and moaned.

"Offer them uppa!" he directed, and then, in a hissing whisper, condemned Jesse and me to death. "S-S-TONNA THEM TOA DUSTA!"

Banging his cracked and chipped ruler, King Bloo rasped in a scratchy voice, "Zis is za rool! Let zis be done!"

Choking on their anger, the crystal throng roared their response as the drums crashed and rolled.

The darkened Guards did an about-face and began to march as one into the press of lightless arms and raging faces.

Scheelite held Pyrope to her body, and Gneiss pulled himself together, bravely placing himself in front of Torri as he faced the angry cries.

"DIS IS ILLEGAL!" he cried passionately.

Jesse knelt before me and placed the pulsing Amber Dragonfly in my hands.

"I saw you, Jesse!" I desperately tried to explain. "I was with you . . . and I could see . . . I could hear . . ."

The cries of the crowd were deafening

"Don't look at them, Maggie," he urged. "Don't look."

"But how . . . you were in the Land of Magma and . . . how, how was I able to see you?"

"I don't know," he replied, holding my hands in his.

"Jesse, I'm sorry! I'm so sorry!" I cried.

The crystal drums were whipping the crowd into a frenzy, and Jesse was a blur through my tears.

"I hated you," I blurted. "I didn't want a younger brother. I wanted you to die, not Mom. I'm so sorry, Jesse!"

Jesse nodded with a small smile. "I hated you 'cause nothing I ever did was good enough," he confided. "I wanted a brother, not a sister."

I had so much I wanted to tell him.

"Everyone always said, 'He's so special,'" I professed. "And you are, Jesse. You are—and I love you."

"I am special," he replied matter-of-factly. "We are all special. I've been telling you that for years. I love you, too, Maggot. Close your eyes."

"What . . . ?"

"Close your eyes," he insisted as the screaming crowd tore jagged rocks from the ground.

"But—"

"Close them." he repeated adamantly, and I knew he didn't want me to see what would happen when the drums stopped.

"Forgive me, Jesse," I cried. "Please forgive me."

"You are my sister; I love you, Maggie," he calmly stated and placed his hand over my face. "Close your eyes."

I was crying like a baby.

"STONE THEM! CRUSH THEM!" the crystal mob roared.

Jesse started talking to me in a normal voice, as if there were no screaming crowd at all.

"Breathe, Maggie . . ." he softly suggested, "breathe in—and breathe out."

I knew the drums were about to stop.

"Watch yourself breathe, Maggie," he directed me.

Somewhere behind my racing heart I could feel my breath pushing me . . . pulling me.

"Listen to their voices," he continued calmly. "Listen. Go inside their roar, Maggie—try to listen to their voices."

I could feel their anger.

"Listen, Maggie—listen!" he urged softly. "Can you see yourself listening?"

"No! I can't hear!" I cried, too afraid now to open my eyes. "I can't see, I can't hear —"

Suddenly Jesse's voice seemed to be coming from *inside* me, clear and strong. "I can't do it without you, Maggie," he insisted.

"Do what? Do what?" I pleaded, the horrible noise reverberating through me.

"Can you see yourself, Maggie?" his voice asked calmly, "Can you see yourself sitting there listening to me?"

The strange thing is that I *could* see us sitting there, and I could see myself listening to Jesse . . . and to the raging mob.

"I'm scared!" I blurted. "I'm too scared!"

"A part of me is scared too, Maggie," his voice whispered through every part of me. "A part of me is scared, Maggie, a part of me—but not *all* of me," he insisted, his voice sounding softer, slower. "Find the part of you that's scared, Maggie. See it. Draw a line around it. See where it begins; see where it ends. Is it in your stomach, your chest? What color is it?"

It must've been some kind of hypnosis because as I was doing it, the roar of the crowd seemed farther off.

"Fear is our *friend*, Maggie," Jesse kept on, sounding like our mother. "It's there to *remind* us to welcome it and thank it for helping us to remember that we have a place where there is *no* fear, a place from which we can love ourselves in our fear . . . love ourselves for how much we want to be brave . . . and to be loved."

I could see myself sitting with my brother holding the light of the Dragonfly Amber, my fear filling my belly and squeezing my heart so that I could hardly breathe. I could see my mind screaming, "Run! Run!"

I could see myself scared and crying. I could see myself thinking of Mommy dying, of Daddy and Jesse, and how we were all scared of being so helpless; how we all had that fear, and how we all wanted to belong.

I could see myself feeling my fear, my sadness, my yearning . . . and suddenly I felt free . . . and light . . . and I knew in my heart that I would always belong in that magical place because it was a part of me and always would be.

I didn't feel alone.

Something hit my shoulder.

The crystal creatures had begun to throw their rocks.

They were stoning us and it felt as if it were happening to someone else. The roar of the crowd was still there, and so was the sound of my breath coming in and rushing out like waves on a beach!

Then I realized that the rock-throwing had stopped.

I opened my eyes.

Everything was so bright—I could barely see.

A brilliant sphere of white light surrounded Jesse and me, and my heart was so full it felt as if it would burst.

Coursing waves of blue-and-white light were washing through Torri, Scheelite, Pyrope, Gneiss, and the people of Chrystallia, who were sighing a rainbow of oohs and aahs.

Dazed by their own brilliance, the Basalt Guards stood frozen like statues.

Lords and Ladies spun and swooned, and the Holy Clear gazed in disbelief at his own body, which was exploding with light.

"H-howa—? H-how issa thissa p-possible?" he stammered.

King Bloo blazed brilliantly as the Green Queen's blossoming hand flew to her throat. "Bloo? Bloo . . . ?" she cried in disbelief. "I'm . . . I'm turning greeen!"

In a riot of raging colors, Torri swept what was left of Pyrite's vibrating cubes up in a neon embrace. "Ooh, you ah sooo priitty," she crooned to Pyrite. "Ah yuh aahll gold?"

Pyrite flashed a staccato of blushes as Torri tossed him like a glittering boa about her neck. "Oh mah!" she shivered. "Oh maahhh . . . OH MAHHH!"

Shimmying and shaking, Lady Topaz and the Obsidian Twins broke into song.

The crystal crowd started dancing as Scheelite, glowing nearly white, dutifully took the Orange Prince's sparkling hand and allowed him to help her to her feet.

"Mon dieu! Yoo are so beaootiful!" he gasped, unable to contain his orange light.

Leaning bashfully into the golden flashes that danced up and down her Bloo's powerful arm, the Emerald Queen gazed adoringly up at the determined set of his jutting blue jaw.

He seemed to be working on a sneeze.

"I—aah—aaAHHH . . ."

Glinting importantly around Torri's neck, Pyrite finally found his mouth and called the glittering Court to attention.

"A r-rool! A r-rool!" he proudly piped.

Tearing his eyes from Scheelite's beauty, the Orange Prince indicated Pyrope with a grand gesture. "Go!" he commanded her, "Go, ma chère! Go to your red-and-white Pyr-rope."

Scheelite couldn't believe her ears.

Neither could Lady Hiddenite, who instantly throbbed a golden yellow and giggled in spite of herself.

Bowing gratefully to the Orange Prince, Scheelite cried out to him, "You will always be my rock!" and ran to Pyrope.

The Orange Prince smiled angelically at Lady Hiddenite. She blushed like a schoolgirl as he knelt before King Bloo, who was getting very blue and closer to his sneeze.

"Papa," the Orange Prince announced with deep humility, "I haff decided to become zee Preest. I ham going eento zee Brozzerhood of Zee Clear," he gargled. Pivoting on his knees to the Holy Clear, he bowed his head and added, "If yoo weel haff my 'umble light?"

Lady Hiddenite's thin jaw dropped in shock, and the Holy Clear's mouth clamped shut so fast that he chipped a diamond tooth.

Speechless, King Bloo chanced a glance at the Queen.

The Cathedral bells began to peal.

Holding Scheelite, Pyrope pointed at Gneiss, who was beside himself with his own brilliance. "You've got sparkle, Mister Gneiss!"

"Look at dis!" Gneiss sputtered to Torri. "I got spahkle!"

She smiled at him, and he got stuck in her gaze, then gallantly offered her his arm.

Shyly, she lowered her eyes and, with a very content expression, took him up on his offer.

Jesse tugged on my sleeve. "Promise that we'll never forget the Princess," he asked gently.

I was so full of love that I wanted to cry. So I did.

"Or Baz," I added.

"Haa—haaa—haaZZAAA—CHOOOOOOO!" sneezed the King.

The ground, the Cathedral, the crystal people—everything— shook as the entire Royal Court stood regally in his wind, and the people of Chrystallia cried out in adoration, "Metabless you! Metabless you! Metabless you! "

HOME

A white blanket of silence and the soft hoot of an owl . . .

I opened my eyes.

I was in my bed! A wave of fear washed over me. Was Mom all right?

It was dark out. What time was it? Had she died? Why had I said those awful things to her last night?

I had to tell her how sorry I was.

Wrapping my jacket around me, I rushed to her room only to discover Jesse standing at the foot of her bed.

What was *he* doing there, I thought, feeling a rush of anger.

Mom's face was nearly swallowed up by her hair in the dim light.

Was she still breathing? Was I too late? Where was Daddy?

Panicked, I was about to call out to her when her eyes fluttered open.

I ducked behind the doorway.

It took a moment for her to see Jesse.

"I had a dream," he whispered.

Smiling, she weakly patted the bed beside her and took Jesse's hand as he sat.

"Tell me."

So Jesse sat on our mom's bed, and I sat on the floor outside her door and listened.

I listened in amazement to Jesse tell about Sedentia, and Chrystallia, the Kingdom of Beryl . . . the Green Queen. I listened to him tell about Fossilia and the Amethyst Princess and the Amber Girl . . .

He was telling my dream! Everything! Every crystal, every person, everything that happened to us . . .

He was telling about how we got split up beneath the old city, and he just stopped talking.

"Jesse . . . ?" Mom asked softly.

He looked scared and lost.

"I can't remember!" he whispered, distraught. He tried

describing what had happened after the rock ledge erupted and separated us, but he couldn't remember.

"Why can't I remember?" he cried.

The wind whipped and the owl hooted once more, and the next thing I knew, I was standing in the doorway.

"I can," I declared in amazement. "I can remember it all."

And I finished telling Jesse's dream.

"We had the same dream!" Jesse blurted.

I nodded, tears running down my cheeks.

Gently pushing the hair from my face, Mom smiled softly. "Well," she replied, "maybe it wasn't a dream."

I took her hand and held it to my heart. How could I ever tell her what I'd learned?

"I understand, Mommy . . . I do. I understand!"

She smiled at me and in that moment, she was younger and more beautiful than I can ever remember.

"I know you do, sweetheart," she whispered " . . . and it's the most wonderful gift you could ever have given me."

Clang . . . clang . . . clang . . . rang the chuck-wagon triangle that Uncle Billy insisted on banging for every meal.

"Merry, Merry Christmas and a Ho-Ho-Ho to all!" he jovially hollered from downstairs. "Breakfast is on!"

Jesse and I helped Dad carry Mom to the couch as Billy clomped out of the kitchen wearing his apron and carrying a tray of steaming cups brimming with hot chocolate. "Cody! Firewood!" he ordered.

Dad seemed distracted as he rushed to put on his jacket. "I'll get it . . . was on my way . . ." he mumbled and headed out.

"Cody?" Uncle Billy barked quietly, trying not to spill the hot chocolate.

"Okay!" Cody moodily replied. He jumped up, threw a log on the fire, and grabbed his boots and followed Dad out the door.

Jesse kept glancing from me to the tree.

I was thinking the same thing. I had to look; I had to see!

"Wow! Look at all the presents!" I exclaimed to Uncle Billy, who smiled proudly.

I ducked behind the tinseled boughs and peeked under the green tree skirt as Jesse appeared around the other side.

There were no roots.

There were several large dark swirls in the grain of the floor that hadn't been there before—swirls where roots might have been.

Mom was watching me with a glint in her eye.

"Let's eat!" Uncle Billy exclaimed, distributing the hot chocolate. "Who's hungry?"

"I'm starved," Jesse lied as he sat down next to Mom.

Brushing the snow from their hair, Daddy and Cody came stomping in. Daddy's eyes were all puffy, like he'd been crying. "Let's open the presents first," he proposed overly enthusiastically, "then I'll whip up some breakfast."

"Already taken care of," Uncle Billy pronounced, eager to have us eat his cooking. "Pancakes with frosted oatmeal!" he announced. "Saw it on the cooking channel. They said, use cereal. I figured, hey, oatmeal is a cereal."

The silence was deafening.

Mom spoke up.

"Your brother loves you, William," she said softly, "but he can't eat your cooking." Then she added gently, "The truth is—none of us can."

There was an uncomfortable pause as Billy slowly nodded,

and Cody and Aunt Doris shared a smile. "Well, why didn't somebody say something?" he replied. "Okay," he announced with a shrug of his shoulders, "I'll be in charge of presents," he declared. "Jesse? Care to help me?" he asked, as he joined Cody on the floor.

Jesse was staring at something in his hand.

"What is it?" I asked.

"It . . . it was in my pocket," he whispered in amazement, holding up a beautiful piece of quartz with pyrope crystals.

"Oh!" I blurted.

Cody peered at it. "Hey! There's a face!"

Uncle Billy took a gander and jokingly declared, "Hey, that looks just like me!"

"I think it looks just like Jesse," Mom whispered with a knowing smile.

Reaching into my pocket, I scratched my knuckle on something hard.

I pulled out a chunk of . . . scheelite?

"Wow! Did you find that in the mine?" Cody asked.

"I thought you weren't supposed to go into the mine,"

Daddy reminded Jesse, taking a closer look at the scheelite. "I can see a face in this one too! It looks like—"

"Maggie?" queried Uncle Billy.

Daddy turned to Mom and gazed into her eyes.

"I was going to say her mom," he whispered softly.

Uncle Billy grunted. "Anybody want more hot chocolate?" he inquired, adding, "It's instant."

"C'mon, you guys," Daddy urged, rubbing his hands together. "Let's do presents."

Tossing Cody a gift, Uncle Billy climbed to his feet. "Here you go, chief. I'm gonna go put on some music."

Jesse couldn't bear the wait. "Are we really going to do one present at a time?"

"No way!" Daddy laughed, shaking his head. "Go on, dig in."

It was a Christmas I shall never forget.

Jesse, Mom, and I sat holding hands on the couch and watched as the others opened their presents. Daddy sat across the room and watched us with this big smile on his face and tears rolling down his cheeks.

Uncle Billy had finally found something he was good at—following Aunt Doris's orders.

Pointing to the top of the tree, Mom whispered in surprise, "Maggie, Jesse . . . look!"

Reflecting off the skylight, a brilliant beam of morning light ignited our crystal angel.

I gazed up at it, wanting, praying, with every part of my being for this moment to never, ever end.

"Mom?" Jesse confided, holding her hand. "Whatever happens, whatever is going to happen, to our house, to us—we love you, and we'll always have your love."

I kissed my mom's cool forehead. "I'm sorry, Mommy," I whispered. "I'm so sorry for being such a baby"—a great sadness welled up through me, and my voice became high and small—"and for saying all those things. I didn't mean . . ."

Gently putting her arm around me, she smiled, and I could feel her strong fingers softly gather me to her. "But you are my baby, sweetheart—and I know you're sorry. I know."

"And Jesse and me—Jesse and I"—silly me; I corrected my bad grammar even as I fought to hold back my tears—"Jesse and I are gonna be okay. Okay? We'll take care of Daddy. I'll take care of Jesse—"

"And I'll take care of Maggie," Jesse interrupted.

I had to resist the urge to roll my eyes and make a "whatever" face.

Mom caught me and smiled knowingly, then shook her head in awe at the two of us. "How did my little boy and beautiful girl become so grown up?" she wondered.

Her eyes sparkled as she pulled us to her. Kissing our brows, she whispered, "We'll have this forever, yes?"

Jesse smiled bravely and nodded his head.

My heart was so full I felt as if I could swim in it.

"Now," she insisted, "go find your presents."

And she gently pushed us off the couch.

A magical shaft of morning sunlight

Shot from dawn's crack in the cloudy horizon.

It ricocheted straight up from our icy skylight

Then disappeared into a universe of falling snow.

"We wish you a Merry Christmas . . ." sang the voices coming from Daddy's stereo, and Uncle Billy's voice declared, "Merry Christmas, everyone! Jesse, this one's got your name on it. Maggie—you're next!"

Millions of snow crystals blew
Every which way in the gusting wind.

"Wow!" exclaimed Cody's voice. "Maggie, where'd you get that?"

"I don't know!" my stunned voice replied. "It was in my other pocket, and . . ."

A swirling funnel of snow
Danced across white drifts.

"It's so beautiful!" trilled Aunt Doris's voice.

"Jesse—?" I squeaked.

"It's amethyst!" blurted Jesse.

The wind washed a flurry of snowflakes
Across the sparkling whiteness.

"Amethyst? It looks like—a person!" Cody observed.

"It looks like . . ." Jesse's voice faltered.

"Princess Amethyst?" I whispered.

"Amethyst is your birthstone," Mom's voice quietly reminded me. "Ancient civilizations prized it over all other gems."

Her voice became the wind.

"The Ancient Egyptians believed it to have the highest vibrations . . ."

Her softness wrapped itself around me
And became one with mine.

". . . which bring forth the purest aspirations of humankind . . ."

And dancing in the morning light
Sparkling swirls of snow chased the night.

". . . and tell us that we are . . ."

A measureless multitude of magical crystals
Scattered and battered by wind and light,

". . . and always will be . . ."

Swooping whispers of fragile flakes in flight
It was she who kept me safe in her arms
And held me tight.

". . . always will be . . .

love."